# OASIS

AJA CORNISH

Oasis Copyright © 2024 Aja Cornish
www.thefinestgems2020@gmail.com

All rights reserved. Without limiting the rights under copyright reserved above. No part of this book may be reproduced, stored in or introduced into a retrieval system, or transmitted in any form, or by any means (electronic, mechanical, photocopying, recording, or otherwise) without prior written consent from the author except brief quotes used in reviews, interviews or magazines.This is a work of fiction. It is not meant to depict, portray or represent any particular real person. All the characters, incidents and dialogue in this written work are the product of the author's imagination and are not to be considered as real. Any references or similarities to actual events, entities, real people living or dead, or to real locations are intended for the sole purpose of giving this novel a sense of reality. Any similarities with other names, characters, entities, places, people or incidents are entirely coincidental.

www.thefinestgems2020@gmail.com
Paperback Books may be purchased @
https://www.thefinestgems.co/

# CONTENTS

| | |
|---|---|
| *Acknowledgments* | v |
| *A Note To My Gem Tribe:* | ix |
| *Disclaimer:* | xi |
| *Preface* | xiii |
| *Proper Pronunciation of Names:* | xv |
| *Musical Interlude:* | xvii |

1. Chapter One — 1
2. Chapter Two — 17
3. Chapter Three — 31
4. Chapter Four — 41
5. Chapter Five — 59
6. Chapter Six — 75
7. Chapter Seven — 95
8. Chapter Eight — 111
9. Chapter Nine — 129
10. Chapter Ten — 141
11. Chapter Eleven — 159
12. Chapter Twelve — 171

| | |
|---|---|
| *Afterword* | 175 |
| *About Author Aja Cornish:* | 177 |
| *Social Media Links:* | 179 |
| *Also by Aja Cornish* | 181 |

# ACKNOWLEDGMENTS

*God You Are Amazing! Thank you for every single talent You have placed inside of me, especially the gift of writing. Thank You for every idea you give me, and the courage to share my heart with the world.*

*There's no way I can let this opportunity pass by without honoring three special gems who made my writing process exceptional. Melvina Locue-Wilson, Lisette Bass, Jalessa Jackson of Jalesareads. The process of working with you ladies was seamless, and lots of fun. To say y'all outdone yourselves is a huge understatement. Thank you just doesn't seem like a big enough word to express the gratitude I feel in my heart. Just know I appreciate all of you. The way you ladies believe in me, push me, and love these characters the same as I do is unmatched.*

*XOXO*

# DEDICATION

*This book is dedicated to all the women out there who know what it is to experience the lows of a relationship. This story was crafted with hope as the intention. Despite living in a world where women have men outnumbered by a long shot, always remember your blessings are tailored. When a man truly wants you, he will pursue you at all cost. You won't have to guess about his motives because he'll be equivalent to an open book. There's an OASIS of love on the horizon, Sis. While you wait, do all it takes to prepare yourself.* 🖤

*"Love is or it ain't. Thin love ain't love at all…"*
~ Toni Morrison

## A NOTE TO MY GEM TRIBE:

*Hey Gems! It's always an honor, and joy to share my God-given gift with all of you. I'm proud of myself and my growth as an author. I've learned to appreciate every lesson, moment of growth, every peak, and valley. I use them all as personal stepping stones, and inspiration to push harder. Quitting has never been a part of my nature. I'm purpose driven. So, those of you who are rocking with me~ Thank you so much. As you know, there is so much more to come. Until then, buckle up & enjoy the ride.*

## DISCLAIMER:

*Please be advised that this book is based in a City that has lived in my imagination for a little over a year now. Groove City, California does not exist in real life. I repeat, Groove City, California doesn't exist in reality. This story is a work of fiction, but gives a sense of reality because of the message left on the pages. In the event you don't care to read about made up places, please STOP right here. If you're okay with the above... Please leave me an honest rating/review when you're done. Thank you, Thank you, Thank you all in advance for taking time out of your schedule to indulge in my art. Until next time...*

*I love all y'all big*

*~AC*

# PREFACE

*Although an Oasis is defined as a fertile spot in the desert, where water is found. It can also be used to describe a peaceful area in our lives. An Oasis of love when found is like a harvest, full of sustenance, safety, and peace.*

# PROPER PRONUNCIATION OF NAMES:

*Beautii- Beauty*
*Bilaal- Bi-laal*
*Blyss- Bliss*
*Fayth-Faith*

MUSICAL INTERLUDE:

There was a woman, her heart was golden, deep as the ocean.
And then this one man, he came and broke it. 'Till it was open, just
like a Lotus. Oh, yes, there were explosions. She found her focus.
The beast was awoken.

~ Jhene Aiko/Lotus

## CHAPTER ONE

### BEAUTII HAMILTON

"Beautii! I'on give a fuck how successful you are. I'm the best you gon' ever get in this life. The fuck? Ain't no upgrade after me," Bilaal declared. "Yo' ass must've forgot who I am! That pussy ain't goin' nowhere."

"Oh, you got me fucked up, my nigga!" Beautii spazzed. "If you're the best I can do, I'm 'bout to be a muthafuckin' nun. Right now, in this very moment," Beautii fumed, and pointed at the ground. "I'm taking back my mind, heart, and my pussy! I know who you are, and who you want to be. They not the same, and I'm done tryna please yo' schizophrenic havin' ass. Get the fuck out my house, and you can keep all them keys; I'm gettin' my locks changed on that ass!" Beautii couldn't believe Bilaal's typical, triflin' ass audacity. He was a prime example of a nigga who did you wrong, then tried to act like shit is sweet.

"That's how you feel, Beautii? You really that mad at a nigga 'cause I took a bitch out to eat, and fucked her one time?" Bilaal asked, as he stared in the face of the woman he loved, but just couldn't seem to do right by. He felt like he could have his cake and eat it too, and Beautii would forever take his bullshit.

"Do you hear yourself right now?" Beautii quizzed. "I'm sick of your shit, nigga. I should have nipped this bullshit ass relationship in the bud a long time ago. I'm done! And, if you bring yo' black ass back here, I'm callin' the cops. I'm not settling for your bullshit no more. I need to focus on myself for once. All you've been is one big ass distraction and tedious headache that frankly, I can do without. Now get the fuck on!"

"Bet! Fuck you, and this apartment. I'm not payin' the rent this month either. I'm sick of yo' ass too," Bilaal replied, but was inwardly salty about Beautii taking things to this extreme.

"Good! Go stay with that bitch you was with!" Beautii yelled, as Bilaal walked out of the door.

Beautii leaned her back against the wall, then slid down to the ground holding the left side of her chest. Her heart beat erratically in her chest, as a stream of fresh, hot tears expelled from her eyes. She was beyond hurt, but deep down there was no confusion in her heart. She desired more. Beautii knew better existed, she just hadn't met the manifestation of it yet. She was finishing out the last year of law school, and had found herself in the midst of a relationship that was destined for shipwreck from the start. Beautii had indulged in a one night stand with Bilaal a year ago, and things between them had dragged out longer than she anticipated.

Bilaal was thugged out and knew how to lay pipe. It didn't help that he was fine as hell either. He was light skinned, sexy lips, and had intoxicating-Hennessy colored eyes. Beautii wasn't the type to allow sex to cloud her judgment; she didn't stay committed to Bilaal for a year because she was dickmatized. It was the deep pain she witnessed in his eyes, and his troubled past that disturbed her good judgment. Beautii's heart lurched when it resonated that Bilaal needed love. Healing. She thought that if she loved him fiercely, he'd reciprocate and love her back. She couldn't have been more wrong. No woman can change a man if he doesn't see the error of his ways.

Bilaal had caught Beautii at a time in her life that she just wanted to live a little and have some fun for once. All she did was study law day in and day out. She was taught commitment and sacrifice at a young age. She wanted it more than anything. She craved success so bad, and Beautii was so close; she could taste it. Her father, Bruce, had been falsely accused, and sentenced to twenty-five years to life in Groove City State Prison one month after she'd been accepted into the *University of California*. Beautii made her father a promise that once she graduated from law school, her first assignment would be to prove his innocence and get him out of prison.

Like the back of her hand, she knew her father's case inside and out. He was her purpose, and when she got weary in well doing; one collect call from her old man made her remember why all her hard work was necessary. Beautii's father was her first love. He'd modeled the perfect example of what a real man looked like, and the proper way to treat a woman. Simply put, she knew better, but wasn't doing better. Beautii wiped her face clean with the palm of her hand, and willed herself to get it together. Bilaal wasn't worth the tears she'd allowed to stream down her face.

*"Never let a man walk through your mind with dirty feet."*

Beautii heard her father's voice in her ear as she remembered one of the many gems he dropped during their talks. *That muthafucka was sent from hell,* Beautii surmised, and blessed the day she'd returned him to sender. Gathering her strength, she rose from the ground, and made her way into the bathroom to run a hot bath. She grabbed her *Dr. Teal's Lavender* epsom salt, and poured it into the water so she could relax.

Once the tub was full, Beautii grabbed her towels, and a few candles to light up and decorate around the tub. Beautii then walked to the kitchen, and poured herself a glass of Roscato Rosso Dolce. *I guess Bilaal's hoe ass was good for something.* Beautii shook her head at her thoughts. Bilaal had bought this bottle of wine for her for her birthday, and it quickly turned into her favorite wine after tasting it once. Halfway out of the kitchen, she doubled back and grabbed the whole bottle. Adele said it best.

*"Sometimes the road less traveled, is a road best left behind."*

These were the exact sentiments of Beautii's heart at the moment as she sipped her glass of wine. The day had already been eventful with school and work. The last thing Beautii had expected was to go pick up dinner from *Red Lobster,* and catch Bilaal out having dinner with one of his side hoe's. She'd made her presence known, then gracefully walked out. The guilt that rode Bilaal's back wouldn't allow him to sit there and digest his food knowing he'd been caught smack dab in the middle of his bullshit. Beautii shook her head at the lingering expectation she harbored for Bilaal to own his fuck-up's. By now she realized that he'd never do that because that would require him to grow up.

*"When you have higher expectations for your life, sometimes you*

*just gotta remove all the clutter from around you. Make room for your blessings."*

Beautii made it a point to make it to class almost twenty minutes early. She chose the seat closest to the window because usually the soft sounds of birds chirping early in the morning soothed her psyche. She gazed out of the window and gnawed on her fingernails as anxiety vigorously surfed through her body. Beautii had done everything possible to prepare herself for the bar exam. Frankly if she didn't have it by now, she wasn't going to get it.

"What's up, girly? Are you ready?" Fayth, Beautii's best friend asked as she sat down at the desk behind her.

"Hell no. I think I'm in over my head," Beautii replied, still trying to settle her nerves.

"Girl, all that studying we've done the last month, and countless sleepless nights; we 'bout to ace this shit. I've already spoken it out in the atmosphere. The universe is on our side," Fayth confidently proclaimed. True to her name, she was full of faith, and Beautii welcomed all the positive energy she could contain in this moment.

"I hope you're right, boo. I'm so ready to move on to the next phase of my life." Beautii took a deep breath, then exhaled all the frisson energy she was experiencing.

In times like this, Beautii thanked God for Fayth. She'd been such a blessing in Beautii's life for the last seventeen years; they'd been besties since the fourth grade. A lifetime only affords you two, maybe three if you're lucky. So far it was Fayth, and Beautii was satisfied. Females were way too shifty and fickle for Beautii's taste. The way her attitude and temper was set up, it was best for everyone.

As the other students started filing in the class, things got real for both Fayth and Beautii. It was time to show and prove.

"Good morning, everyone," Mrs. Baxter energetically announced, with an infectious smile. She took pride in her job, and was confident that she'd poured everything into her students to be successful.

"Good morning," A few voices chimed in throughout the classroom as everyone got situated in their seats.

Terilyn, Mrs. Baxter's daughter and assistant walked down each aisle and passed out the test and coding sheets; while Mrs. Baxter gave the last announcements and instructions for the test.

*Three Months Later…*

Beautii drove three hours to make it to her interview with Blyss Valentino. She'd put in an application to work with him one month prior to receiving a response from his assistant, Jillian. *Lord, I need your help.* Beautii silently prayed as she walked confidently through the doors of Regal Valentino Law office. She was still a little nervous, but if she had to bet on anyone; she'd always bet on herself.

"Good morning. How are you?" Beautii greeted the front desk clerk with a warm smile, her voice carrying a hint of enthusiasm.

"You must be Beautii Hamilton. I'm Jillian," she said, reaching her hand forward for Beautii to shake.

"I am. It's an honor to be considered to work with such a prestigious law office." Beautii humbly stated, as she looked around the fine establishment.

"With your GPA and high scores on the bar exam, you could have chosen to go anywhere in the world to practice law. The fact that you graduated a year early, and had the highest scores in your entire class, placed you in a class of your own." Jillian told her honestly. "We are honored that you want to partner with us. We only accept the best candidates here."

"Of course," Beautii agreed, and admired the simple, yet crisp, and classy decorations. Brown, antique white, and gold was the color scheme choice. Beautii loved it so much, she could already see herself coming to work every day, and she wasn't even hired yet.

"Right this way," Jillian said, as she tapped Attorney Blyss Valentino's door.

"Come in," Blyss welcomed Jillian inside, as he already anticipated Beautii's presence.

"It's a great day in Groove City now that you're here," Blyss charmingly stated, as he rose from his seat and offered his hand for Beautii to shake.

"It's a pleasure to meet you," Beautii replied, and clasped her hand in a firm handshake. "I'm honored to be here," she added with an infectious smile.

"I'll be right out front. If you need anything please let me know." Jillian informed the duo, then walked out and closed the door behind herself.

"Now that all the formalities are out of the way, let's get down to business. Shall we?" Blyss stated seriously with a warm undertone laced in his voice. Smooth. Sexy. Sensual. Blyss was a consummate, unrivaled, professional, and in a class of his own. He had captured and mesmerized Beautii the moment he locked eyes with her without an ounce of effort.

"We shall," Beautii attentively agreed. She struggled to

yank her mind out of the gutter; however, she managed when she thought about what was most important.

"Tell me what it is that drew your attention to this law office in particular?" Blyss asked, as he leaned back in his chair, and overlapped one hand over the other.

Beautii took a deep breath and rubbed her moist lips together before answering. "Aside from the fact that you're one of the best black lawyers in California, and have won every case you've ever represented; your mission statement won me over."

"The mission statement?" Blyss was intrigued because Beautii was the first person who'd ever given him this answer. Most candidates wanted to join his law firm because they wanted to know who his connections were, or they just wanted to be able to add his firm on their resume. It would guarantee them a job anywhere in the United States. "What exactly was said that won you over?" Blyss needed to know.

"I believe it was the part where you elaborated on how everyone deserves a second chance. You spoke on how important it was to give a voice to black men and women who were guilty before innocence had a chance to prevail." The words spilled from Beautii's lips with conviction. A lot of lawyers were just in this line of business because of the money, and they could care less about innocence or guilt. Beautii could tell the statement came from a genuine place, and couldn't ask for anything more. Things like character, real justice, and equality meant something to Beautii. Knowing she'd be working with someone who held some of the same morals as she did went a long way with her.

Blyss nodded his head, then licked his lips. "When can you start?"

"I'll need time to find a place and get settled in," Beautii replied, trying her best to restrain her excitement. "Can you give me two months?" She asked.

"I have a house you can rent from me for as long as you want. It's already furnished, and all the appliances are brand new and up to date." Blyss offered, as he shifted his attention to his computer screen and started typing.

"Wow, that's extremely generous of you. I don't know… Can I see it first?" Beautii fumbled over her words, unclear on if she should accept or decline.

Blyss turned his apple screen around to face Beautii. "Here's a complete view of the house from top to bottom." Blyss slowly scrolled through forty detailed pictures with Beautii then asked, "So what do you think? Is this up to your high expectations?" Blyss smiled convincingly, making it impossible for Beautii to say no.

"I don't know what to say," Beautii was out done with Blyss' generosity.

"Say yes," Blyss winked. You'll be the first besides me to step foot in there to live. Make it your own."

"How much?" Beautii needed to know because her funds weren't the best. Her mind was running one hundred miles a minute trying to figure out how she'd make the transition.

"I'll tell you what, the first six months are free. That should give you enough time to stack some bread. Then we'll come together again and discuss a fair price for rent." Blyss munificently offered, and hoped she'd accept. Blyss had purchased it brand new a year prior, and still hadn't found a suitable occupant for his property yet. "I'll draw up some paperwork and make it more official, but in the meantime, here's a gas card to take care of your gas, and any other expenses you may have to make your transition seamless." Blyss handed Beautii his business card and waited for her acceptance.

"Thank you so much for all you're doing for me. I promise to give one-hundred and twenty percent to being an asset to your team," Beatii assured as she reached forward to accept the card.

"I know you will. Just give me a call when you get back. I'll have the papers drawn up, and your keys will be here waiting for you."

"You're a God-send. Thank you so much."

*Three Weeks Later...*

"I told you, Beautii. When you do your part, God will do his. Don't allow nothing or nobody to break your peace, or sway your focus," Beautii's father encouraged her just as he'd always done. Even behind bars, he remained her favorite, and she maintained her position as her daddy's girl.

"You're always right daddy. You've never told me anything wrong." Beautii agreed. "I can't wait to come see you again, especially now since I'll be a lot closer."

"It'll do my heart some good to lay eyes on you too. How's your mother doing?" Beautii's father inquired. He called her three times a week, and the last time he'd called her, she'd broke down and cried. It broke his heart because like her, he wanted to be close to her as well. He vowed to make it all up to her once Beautii proved his innocence.

"You know we have to take it one day at a time with her. She misses you so much daddy. She's doing alright though." Beautii told him honestly. Contrary to what people thought, telling the truth would forever be the best way to go. She never softened the blow for her father, no matter how bad the news was. He appreciated her for it.

"I know. I know. Just help me keep her encouraged. It won't be long now that you've partnered with the best lawyer in Groove City, and found favor with him." Beautii's father mildly boasted and encouraged himself at the same time.

"You have thirty seconds remaining," the operator chimed in and interrupted their conversation.

"That's my time Beautii, I love you."

"I love you too, daddy. As soon as I get situated, I'll be mailing you some paperwork."

"Sounds good. I'll talk to you later."

"Mwahh," Beautii sent her father an air kiss.

"I got you," her father replied before ending the call.

Beautii took a moment to vibe with Jhene Aiko as she sang *Speak*. She'd prayed, pressed, and persisted until she finally walked into her season of harvest. Whoever said when you elevate, people drop out of your life, like water from a duck's back told the truth. Everybody can't stick around when you enter the best parts of your life, that's why God shows you their true colors before you get there. Despite life's ups and downs, Beautii counted her blessings, and named them one by one often. She'd witnessed a lot of her peers fall by the wayside for one reason or another, and Beautii refused to be a statistic. She never missed a day when it came to taking her birth control, and as much as she loved Bilaal; she didn't allow him to disrupt her flow when it came to her priorities. The chiming of Beautii's phone caught her attention instantly. Reaching over to her nightstand, Beautii answered on the third ring.

"Hey girl, heyy!" Beautii excitedly exclaimed.

"Hey baby boo! Tell me something good," Fayth replied with matched excitement. They hadn't had much of an opportunity to chat since they had passed the bar exam.

"You'll never guess who I'll be working side by side with," Beautii stated, then bit down on her bottom lip.

Fayth took a moment to think it over before responding. "Girl, shut up! I know you lying."

"What? I haven't said a word yet." Beautii chuckled at her best friends' dramatics.

"Did you get the job with Blyss Valentino?"

"Yes! I'll be starting next month," Beautii happily revealed.

"That's amazing news, boo! I'm so happy to hear that. I know how bad you wanted to work with him. You're gonna learn so much. Watch and see," Fayth said genuinely. She was truly happy for Beautii, and wanted nothing but the best for her.

"I know you have some good news for me too. Come on and spill the tea," Beautii pressed, then propped her left foot under her as she sat in the bed.

"I'm moving to Los Angeles to work with Attorney Theresa Stith." Fayth revealed with a huge smile.

"What?! Fayth, are you serious? That is a once in a lifetime opportunity. That's great!" Beautii genuinely supported her friend, and was happy that she'd stepped out on faith. Attorney Theresa Stith was the only black female lawyer in Los Angeles who had never lost a case no matter what courtroom she stepped foot in. She and Blyss had partnered in a case two years prior that was massive, and they slayed in that courtroom like no other. Beautii and Fayth had followed the case and witnessed every detail first hand. It was the same case that caused them to get a one hundred percent on one of their projects they did together. The amount of case law they had to learn for that one trial wasn't for the faint.

*Knock… Knock… Knock…*

Beautii turned down her music to make sure she wasn't hearing things. When the second round of knocks sounded at the door, she scrunched her face up wondering who could possibly be at her door; she wasn't expecting anyone. Grabbing her phone and sliding her feet in her slides, she made her way to the door.

"Who is it?" She called out loud enough for whoever was on the other side of the door to hear her.

"It's me, baby. Open the door," Bilaal replied sweetly.

*What the fuck is this nigga at my door for? I told him we were done.* Beautii sighed deeply, not in the mood for Bilaal's bullshit.

"What do you want, Bilaal?" Beautii said dryly as she opened the door.

"Can I come in?" Bilaal asked sadly, pining for sympathy. He'd missed Beautii and felt bad about how things had gone down between them the last time they parted ways. Beautii was the love of his life, he just took her presence in his life for granted. In the back of his mind, he felt like she'd always be there. Beautii had made him feel like she'd always be there, and she was until she reached her breaking point.

"Bilaal, I really rather you go on with your life. I don't have time to do this with you today. Just accept that-"

"A nigga ain't gotta accept shit I'on agree wit'. I know I fucked up but damn. Can you forgive me? You know I'm sorry," Bilaal mannishly said, voice dripping with everything but sincerity. "I thought this love shit was supposed to be unconditional. I know you love me, and I love you too. Let's just start over, baby. I miss you." Bilaal moved in closer, and attempted to rest his hands on Beautii's arms.

"Uhn uhn, nigga! Find you another dummy to manipulate," Beautii snatched her arms out of his grasp, and snapped. "You're right about one thing though. I did love you, but not the way I thought I did. Love is unconditional, but your existence in my life had an expiration date. Your actions proved that to me, and I don't need a replay of what I know, and saw with my own eyes. You were full of shit then, and you're full of it now."

"A'yo, who the fuck you talkin' to like that?" Bilaal moved in closer to Beautii once again. "Don't talk to me like I'm a bad nigga 'cause I did a lot of good shit for you. Everyday wasn't bad. Fuck you mean? I was good to you."

Beautii's facial expression softened a bit before she responded. "Just because you were good to me, doesn't mean you were good for me. You weren't a good fit, and I regret that I wasn't able to come to terms with that fact sooner." Beautii said softly, as she spoke the truth from her heart. She had to keep it real with herself first, and because she did, she was able to do the same with Bilaal.

"Mannn," Bilaal dragged. "I see you still on that bullshit. You got my number, call me when you ready to make up wit' a nigga." Bilaal turned to walk out of the door, and caught a glimpse of two boxes Beautii had in the corner of her living room. "Where the fuck you goin'?" Bilaal quizzed abruptly, as he faced Beautii. He peered into her eyes with so much contempt, his eye lids jumped.

"I don't owe you any explanations concerning my whereabouts. We're not in a relationship anymore," Beautii rolled her eyes and replied dismissively. "And your false sense of concern for me is overrated. See yourself out."

"Don't fuckin' play with me, Beautii. I'm not askin' yo' ass again."

Beautii was a lawyer; therefore, it wasn't easy for her to shy away from an argument. In this case she understood that she had already won, so going back and forward would only prolong an unnecessary exchange between them. She opted out. "I'm moving."

Beautii's words knocked the wind out of Bilaal. His hardened eyes turned glassy, as he released a shaky breath. He parted his lips to speak, but no sound came out. The reality of his defeat was transparent, and the walls that Beautii had built around herself were impossible to penetrate. He'd lost her, and there was nothing he could do about it.

"You got anotha nigga don't you?!" Bilaal spat with venom, envy, and jealousy seeping through his pores. "I know damn well, you can't afford to make no drastic move nowhere. Not when I was paying all the bills in this muthafucka."

Beautii giggled a bit. "Get the fuck out my house. I'm not telling you shit about how I'm moving. You wasn't worried about it when you was running the streets, and living a double life. Did I badger you about what the fuck you were doing? I ignored all the red flags, and gave you chance after chance to get your shit together. You didn't, so take your lick and keep stepping. Love don't live here no more."

"Just like that, huh?" Bilaal swiped his thumb across his nose and sniffed away his sadness, then nodded his head accepting what he couldn't control. "Be easy. I'll see you around." Bilaal told her then left after securing the door behind him.

Trey Songz *Fumble* oozed smoothly through the small speakers of Beautii's cell phone. She let out a deep sigh as reality settled in her heart and mind. It was time for her to start the next chapter of her life, and fortunately, it didn't involve Bilaal. Beautii was ready to see the demonstration of all the joy, success, abundance, and peace she'd been seeking with every step she took moving forward.

*"You only get one shot at life. Make sure you don't fumble when the ball is in your court."*

Once again, Beautii's father had been her voice of reason. The remembrance of his words centered her when she needed him most. Bilaal had fumbled Beautii's heart multiple times. This time, she simply didn't have the desire to put herself through giving him a chance to hurt her again. All the opportunities she had given him in the past was the main reason she felt like he didn't respect, or value her now. Beautii owned her part in the dysfunction of their relationship, that's why she had no regrets with the decision she was making. Beautii decided to irrevocably bet on herself going forward.

## CHAPTER TWO

### BLYSS VALENTINO

"You always leave right after we make love to each other," Amor tried to convince Blyss while playing in her honey pot. "We've been playing this strictly sex game for the last six months. I need more now, and I know you feel the vibes too."

Blyss laughed at Amor's little speech while shaking his head. "Feel? The only thing I like to feel when I'm with you, is my nut rising when I'm 'bout to cum in that condom I just flushed down the toilet." Blyss told her straight as he slid his boxer briefs up his toned legs. "I was honest with you about my stance in this entire rendezvous, no?" Blyss turned his attention to face Amor with a raised brow.

"Yes, but things change. You can't possibly think making love to me consistently wouldn't spark some type of feelings within me," Amor said on the verge of making herself cum again. Usually, this would have ignited another round between the two of them, but Amor had turned him completely off with her confession.

"I've never made love to you, Amor. I fuck you, and we

both get off with an understanding that things never go any further between us. I've never led you to believe I wanted anything more." Blyss bent down to grab his sweats off the floor, quickly pulling them up. "The non-disclosure I had you sign should have confirmed my intentions, and silenced any reasonable doubt within you." Blyss continued to get dressed so he could leave.

"Mmmm, shittt…" Amor climaxed, and Blyss watched as her essence oozed out like water from a water fountain.

*Damn.* Blyss thought to himself as he pulled his white tee over his head, and slipped both his feet into his Jordan's. He knew when he walked out of Amor's house, he'd never return again. Blyss wasn't the type of man that played around when it came to matters of the heart. His had been broken once, many moons ago. He wasn't in the business of dogging women out, which was the sole purpose of making all women he messed with sign a disclosure. It hadn't been the first time a woman had caught feelings for him, but when they did, he cut contact before they had a chance to deepen. Blyss was the typical man who could have sex repeatedly with a woman without making any real connection with her. He was extremely selective, and discerning when it came to the women he crossed the line with for numerous reasons. The main one being, he had way too much to lose.

Amor was one of his selections because she too was a lawyer, and understood the lifestyle and risks that were associated with being sloppy. She respected things like contracts, disclosures, and other legal documents. Therefore, anything she was feeling in the heat of the moment would swiftly fly out the window when she came down from the trip Blyss' dick sent her on, and back to her senses. Amor was a gorgeous woman who had enough curves to make the average man dissociate with logic, but Blyss wasn't an average man.

Grabbing his keys off the dresser, he turned around to face Amor and said. "Take care of yourself. It's been real."

Moments later, Blyss stepped up on the running board of his black Escalade ESV platinum, his music pumped with ease through his 36 premium speakers. Bobbing his head to one of his favorite artists' songs immediately put him into a different headspace.

Blyss was thirty-two and loved living a bachelor lifestyle. He came and went as he pleased without having to answer to anyone about his whereabouts, or who he entertained during his free time. He worked hard Monday through Friday, which had afforded and earned him the right to play as hard as his heart desired. Aside from his sexual appetite, he played a major role in the lives of the youth in Groove City, California. As Blyss rode down the street, he noticed a few young men that he'd taken under his wing standing in front of the Nipsey mural that was situated on the side of the brick building. Even though Nipsey had died in Los Angeles, California; he still had a lot of love in Groove City.

*"Double up. Three or four times, I ain't tellin' no lies, I just run it up. Never let a hard time humble us. Double up."*

The young men were all out there selling water and vibing to Nipsey's *Double Up*. They all had a different story, different struggle, but the same need. Money. Surviving against the odds and doing all they could not to become a statistic was a daily strive. Twelve was always somewhere lurking trying to find a reason to start shit. All cops weren't bad, but the ones who were, played a part in the killing of a thirteen year old boy named Tiny Mike. After his death, Blyss made it his business to purchase the youngsters a seller's permit as a way of giving back and honoring Tiny Mike's life.

"What's good, Blyss!" Quette, one of the youngsters rose from the milk crate he was sitting on and asked as he walked towards Blyss' rolled down window on the passenger side.

"You already know what it is my dude, it's slow motion. Tryna make it do what it do," Blyss replied simultaneously meeting Quette's hand with a fist bump. "Howz business comin'?"

"I can't complain, everything steady. You know I'ma hustla at heart, I'ma always make some shit shake." Quette confidently answered, swiping his hand over the top of his head with a savvy smile.

Blyss nodded his head, feeling exactly where Quette was coming from because he too had a hustlers mentality. Without it, he never would have been able to fund his own way through college or grad school. He came from a two parent, middle class household. Unfortunately, his parents weren't able to pay his way through college, and still survive. The goals Blyss had for himself, going to a community college wasn't going to cut it. He needed fast money and the only way he'd get it was by selling drugs. What separated him from becoming a statistic was the fact that he had a plan. He had an end game goal, and he never lost sight of it.

"Here go something for you," Blyss reached in his pocket and handed Quette a stack.

"Good lookin' out, B. Hol' up," Quette told Blyss as he doubled back to grab a few water bottles. "Stay hydrated man. It's hot as hell out here."

"I got you, man. Be sure to stay out the way and focus on ya' bread," Blyss encouraged, knowing how easy it was to get distracted.

"Fa'sho," Quette gave Blyss another hand bump before posting back up on the wall.

Thirty minutes later, Blyss had pulled into his gated community situated in the best suburban area in Groove City. It was every residents' dream to one day own a home in this amazing community. His u-shaped driveway and manicured lawn was something to admire. The flower beds were astonishing, and the gold V on the front of the pillar had lights, and a waterfall streaming from it into a mini pond which gave his mansion a classic feel. Blyss paid eighty-eight million dollars for his thirty thousand square foot home two years ago. It was well worth it for 1.5 acres of land it tastefully sat on and the peaceful overview of water behind the massive estate. Blyss didn't have any kids, but imagined the day he started having them, and decided he'd need a big enough home for everyone to fit comfortably. Eight bedrooms, eleven bathrooms, premium amenities, four pools, fifteen car garage, and bulletproof windows were just a few features that drew him in. His home was immaculate to say the least.

Immediately after letting himself in, he disarmed his alarm, then secured the locks. He sighed deeply after hearing the chiming of his phone. He hadn't even been inside his home for five minutes, and already somebody was calling him. Fishing his phone out of his sweats, he smiled genuinely at the appearance of Beautii Hamiltons' name sliding across his screen.

"Hello. This is Blyss Valentino," He answered on the second ring.

"Good Afternoon, this is Beautii Hamilton. I hope I didn't catch you at a bad time." Beautii replied as she turned down her music a little lower and switched lanes.

"It's not a bad time. What can I do for you?" Blyss asked, then continued his stride deeper into his home.

"I know I told you that I'd likely start moving next week, but I decided not to prolong the process," Beautii revealed, biting down on her bottom lip.

"Is that right?" Blyss asked. "When can I expect you then?" Blyss stopped in the kitchen and grabbed a yellow apple and took a big bite of it.

"Today. I'm about an hour and a half away."

"That's what's up. I'll text you the address, and I'll meet you there with the key and the contract."

"Sounds great. Thank you again for this."

"It's nothing, we're partners. I got cha." Blyss told her, brushing off how grand the gesture was he'd offered her.

"Okay. See you soon," Beautii said before disconnecting the call.

---

Blyss had been waiting in the car for about fifteen minutes before Beautii pulled in the parking space beside him. Turning down her music, then shutting her car off, she slowly got out of her car, then waited for Blyss to meet her on the sidewalk. Beautii was a ball of nerves on the inside. She didn't know if hugging Blyss would be appropriate or not, but she felt indebted to him for being so kind to her.

Grabbing the folder that lay on the passenger seat, Blyss got out of his car and greeted Beautii respectfully. "Good evening, it's good to see you again."

"The honor is all mine," Beautii returned, unable to control her eyes from scanning Blyss' physique. He was tall, slim, and had a golden bronze complexion. His eyes. His energy. His demeanor. Beautii instantly understood why he intimidated so many in the courtroom. Beyond that, the softness in his eyes told her she was safe.

"You ready for your first official walk through?" Blyss broke the silence and asked.

"I am. Let's go," Beautii replied and smiled sweetly.

Together they walked side-by-side until they made it to the front door. Blyss disengaged the locks, disarmed the alarm system, then opened the door wide enough for Beautii to walk through ahead of him. The delicate sound of Beautii's breath getting caught in her throat, caused a smile to spread across Blyss' face. It did his heart good to witness Beautii's joy filled reaction. This was who Blyss Valentino was though, he found pleasure in making the people around him happy and comfortable; especially his colleagues. He was taught early that it's better to give than receive.

Beautii was speechless, as her eyes swept through the entire first floor. It was fully furnished just as it appeared in the pictures, and a complete open floor plan on the first level. The living room was situated on her left, and the kitchen was to her right. Straight ahead led to the stairs. There were a few doors down the hall just past the stairs that she instantly remembered was the half bathroom and storage closet. The pictures Blyss had emailed her of the house were very detailed, but didn't do the place enough justice. Without a word, she examined what was now her newest haven. The fresh flow of tears that streamed down her face served as a refresher. She witnessed the evidence of an oasis she'd been manifesting for a long time. She was speechless, but her face beamed with joy.

Home. It had been a very long time since Beautii had that warm feeling of home; like she was where she needed to be at the right time. She'd been on her own since the day she was accepted into college, but it was no comparison to the moment she had manifested. It hit differently when a person aligned with their destiny opposed to doing what was necessary for survival. Truthfully, this is exactly what Beautii had done. She had been surviving, but now she could live and walk out her true purpose. She didn't expect to become emotional, but it had been a long time coming.

"I love this place," Beautii finally found her voice. "Thank you so much."

"It's yours for as long as you want it to be. To be honest, I don't really have any use for it," Blyss stated while gazing out of the distant bay window. "Here's the paperwork. You can look it over, and give it back Monday morning when you come into the office. For now, let me help you unload." Blyss winked his eye at Beautii, then turned to walk back out the front door.

Beautii took her time as she journeyed through the rest of the condo before going out to help Blyss with the things she brought with her. Stepping into the master boudoir, the only bedroom in the condo that she couldn't see clearly from the pictures taken; she was blown away. From the high ceiling and fancy chandelier, shiny hardwood floor, to the glamorous comforter set that gave the room such an elegant, rich feel. Shades of taupe, beige, créam, brown, and splashes of gold added a feeling of pureness and virtue. Beautii's condo was lowkey situated in one of the high points of Groove City. Quickly she realized there was a view in every room.

"Do you want me to sit these boxes in here, or the guest room?" Blyss asked as he stood by the doorframe.

"Umm, yes. That'll be fine. Thank you," Beautii answered, snapping out of her self- infused trance, then stepped into the ensuite. Her dreams had turned into reality. "Wow," she whispered to herself. Everything was assembled, and fashionably organized.

"You like it?" Blyss asked, and startled Beautii by accident. He'd crept up so quietly she didn't hear him when he entered behind her.

"Whew," Beautii jumped as she turned around holding her chest.

"My bad, Beautii. I didn't mean to scare you."

"Yes. I love it. Did you design all of this yourself?" Beautii needed to know.

"Nah, I hired an interior designer to do it for me. My life is way too busy to be decorating houses," Blyss chucked. "I just told them how I wanted it to feel."

"And what feeling was that?"

"What's understood doesn't need an explanation. You felt it when you walked through the door, and you feel it right now."

"Job well done."

Blyss was right. Beautii was consumed with so much peace, it surpassed her logic. Solace was a thing many sought after, but never fully obtained. The rich used their wealth thinking they could pay for it like everything else, only to find out it couldn't be bought. Peace is priceless. Valuable. A high commodity in a world that's so chaotic and hateful. Beautii took a deep breath, then proceeded forward to help Blyss bring in the rest of her things.

Unapologetically, Beautii beheld Blyss' muscles flex with each box he lifted. Sexy. Strong. Captivating. Beautii was captivated as she peeped all this unbeknownst to him. He owned a class of his own. Power was an attribute that didn't need to make a lot of noise. When you had money, flossing was childish; but make no mistake- there was no mistaking it once observed. Blyss was undoubtedly a powerful man, his presence was felt. Surprisingly, once Beautii made it outside, her car had been unhooked from the U-haul, and Blyss had lifted the last box and brought it in the house. As Blyss ascended the stairs, Beautii found herself drawn to the ray of light that shone in through the window.

Moments later, Blyss descended the steps and made his way to the front door. "Anything else I can do for you before I leave?" Blyss inquired as he looked to his left, and found Beautii standing in front of the bay window observing the distant water view.

Slowly slipping out from the peaceful trance Beautii found herself in the midst of, she turned around to face Blyss. "Yes. That'll be all. Thank you again, I appreciate all you've done.

"Not a problem at all," Blyss dismissed. "When do you have to have the U-haul back?"

"Tomorrow before noon."

"There's no use of puttin' off for tomorrow what we can accomplish today. Come on," Blyss gestured with his hand. "I'll drive the U'haul and you can trail me. Tomorrow you can chill instead of being bothered with unnecessary tasks." Blyss grabbed the key off the console table, then walked out the door.

"This is my partner. He is off limits for anything else that's not business related," Beautii coached herself as she followed Blyss' lead.

YoungBoy's *We Poppin* streamed loudly through the speakers of Endless Summer Breeze, a lounge Blyss and his homeboy's Chief, Flex, and Screw frequented on occasion when they wanted to chill and have a good time. Blyss' day had proved to be an eventful one due to the chain of events that led up to his night out with the fellas. It wasn't often that Blyss got a chance to chill, and explore the new amenities the nightlife Groove City had to offer. When he did, it was always upscale and private.

"Aye' man, before I forget. You heard about that nigga Trevin from around the way?" Chief quizzed, referencing their high school classmate.

With squinted eyes, Blyss jogged his memory. "Trevin Louis?"

"Yea man. He got hemmed up a few weeks ago," Chief disclosed. "Sent word out that he needed representation, and money wasn't an issue." Chief said suggestively.

Blyss nodded his understanding. "Oh yeah?"

"You tryna jump on that?" Chief asked.

"I'll look into it and see what's goin' on." Blyss kept it short and sweet. He wasn't one to agree quickly to anything without all the facts. He prided himself on winning all his cases, and one thing was certain; Trevin Louis was a known Kingpin in Groove City. Whatever evidence and charges the feds had on him was likely valid and would stick.

"Mhm. Look who just walked through the door," Flex announced, then nodded toward the entrance. The fellas were ducked off in the VIP section, but had a clear view of everything coming and going out of the establishment.

"Sedora, Karen, Tammy, and Lanesha," Screw lustfully broadcasted, ready to make his move.

"Damn man, I ain't seen Karen in a long time," Chief said, biting down lightly on his bottom lip.

"Sedora Ryan," Blyss mumbled, lowly, but the fellas heard him. The last time she'd graced him with her presence, he'd fucked her silly, while she made love faces, and screamed his name. She was one of Blyss' favorites because she abided by his rules, played her position, and never breached their contract. It was almost like Sedora heard Blyss' thoughts. She looked up, and their eyes met instantly. As if Sedora could read Blyss' thoughts, a seductive smile spread across her face. Her naughty thoughts mixed with his incited an interestingly, wild night. Neither of the two would back down or walk away from such pleasure. Truth be told, Sedora came hoping to run into Blyss.

Nodding his head in Sedora's direction was enough to let her know, he was on whatever time she was on. As she made her way deeper into the establishment, she got her girls' attention before they found a table, changing their direction, and causing them to look up to the VIP section. Following the direction Sedora pointed at, excitement filled her friends as they followed her lead. Tammy had her eyes on Screw, Karen had been playing hard to get - but she wanted Chief in the worst way. While Flex and Lanesha had been playing the cat and mouse game for years.

"Fine ass, Karen!" Chief greeted as the ladies entered their section. "What up, ma?" He openly flirted as he always did when he saw her. He loved to make her blush.

"Hey, Chief. How you doin'?" She asked, taking the seat right beside him. "It's been a while."

"Yo' lil' ass is somethin' else," Chief chuckled because she knew as well as he did that his face was buried in her pussy two weeks ago.

"Heyyy Screw!" Tammy walked over to him and gave him a hug.

"Aye', we'll be back." Screw told the crew. "Let me holla at you right quick," Screw reached for Tammy's hand, and led the way towards another section.

Like magnets, Flex and Lanesha were drawn to each other. Flex ordered Lanesha a drink, then fell into natural conversation with her. Everyone knew they had something going on, but for their own reasons they hadn't made anything official between them.

Blyss shook his head. "Look at all these love birds. What's goin' on stranger?" Blyss asked Sedora as she took the seat next to him.

"I should be asking that," Sedora pointed her finger in the center of Blyss' chest, and dragged it downward, stopping just above his belt buckle. "You're the one who's been ducking me." Sedora replied seductively, indirectly referencing their last rendezvous. "I've called you twice since the last time we were together." Sedora crossed her legs, and waited for his response.

"Damn. My bad, ma. You know how busy life can get," Blyss dismissed. "I'm right here now though. What's good?" Blyss refused to beat around the bush. There was no need, Sedora knew what time it was between them. "You tryna end the night wit' a good time, or not?" Blyss quizzed with a raised brow, silently daring her to decline his offer.

A flirtatious smile spread across Sedora's face before she answered. Taking a sip of her cocktail, she nodded her head and said, "Of course."

What started out as a men's night out quickly shifted the moment these ladies stepped in and stole the show. There was something about a woman who was confident, knew what she wanted, and didn't play games that turned Blyss on. His life was hectic enough. Stressful enough. He didn't have time to entertain anyone who was on a lower frequency. He and Sedora had the same expectations, which is why their understanding was so solid. It's what made everytime they were together a great experience.

Blyss tilted his head slightly to the right, observing Sedora's body language. Once he interpreted her vibe, it was decided in that instant that it was time to get their night started early.

"Aye, we 'bout to be out, Chief," Blyss announced, rising from his seat, and offering his hand towards Sedora to help her out of her seat. "I'ma hit you up later, a'ight."

"I already know what time it is. We 'bout to shake the spot too. Be easy," Chief caught Blyss' hand, and dapped him up before he left.

"A'ight man," Flex said, dapping Blyss up next. "We gotta do this shit again soon."

"Fa'sho," Blyss agreed, then left discreetly with Sedora on his arm. There was no need for him to wait around for Screw, everybody knew he was gone by now. It was his signature move when he and Tammy got together.

"I see you ain't wasting no time tonight, huh?" Sedora giggled.

"You know me. I'm good at time management, but even better with anatomy."

# CHAPTER THREE

## BEAUTII HAMILTON

*Time to get your head in the game,* Beautii coached herself as she prepared to put her best foot forward as Blyss Valentino broke down the nitty-gritty logistics of their upcoming case. Beautii absorbed every word with razor-sharp focus. She had always known being a good, successful lawyer wasn't a solo show, but as she listened attentively, it was confirmed and made abundantly clear how each branch of their team relied on the other.

"Got anything concrete against our client?" Beautii's voice cut through the air, her pen already dancing across the page, hungry for information.

Blyss glanced over his notes before responding, his tone measured. "A firearm was uncovered, and we've got a quartet of witnesses itchin' to sing against our client. Discovery gon' be creepin' up real quick, so we gotta be ready to play hardball." Blyss confirmed after checking his notes, his demeanor calm yet commanding.

Blyss fought to maintain his professional facade, but Beautii's allure was so siren, refreshing, and so beautiful it was impossible to ignore. His mind told him no, but his dick leapt every time he saw her strut past him with her plump ass. Despite his best efforts, her every move, every curve, sent a primal jolt through him. His heart sat on ice because women were often the most treacherous creatures. Blyss didn't sense bad vibes with Beautii, but there was this look in her eyes that warned him not to play with her. He sensed her complexities and this look urged him to proceed with caution, and unravel her mysteries at a slow pace.

Little did Blyss know, his instincts were spot-on when it came to Beautii. She'd been through some things and the residue of her past still lingered, showing up in her shadows, and hovering over her like grey clouds. There were unresolved scars, lingering traumas that begged for release. Until she learned to extend herself grace, no matter how much success she experienced a void would still reside deep within. Outward beauty and inward turmoil was equivalent to oil and water; it'd never mesh. Until she found peace within herself, the turbulent undercurrents beneath her polished exterior would continue to threaten her equilibrium, a silent storm waiting to break.

"Can I go with you to observe the discovery?" Beautii asked, looking up from her notes.

Yearning. The connection and yearning that emitted from them was so perfuse every time their eyes locked. It was as if time was on their side, and whatever it took for them to get to the oasis they both desired and longed for; the possibilities were limitless.

Leaning back in his chair, Blyss struggled to slow his pulse, but managed. "That'll be fine. How's everything coming along with your workload?"

Beautii sighed deeply.

"Everything is going great, it's just this one case that I'm working on. There's so many moving parts and technicalities, my head had been spinning for days. But, I'm determined to get it right."

"Who's case are you working on? Do you have it with you?"

"It's my father's case. I have everything in my office."

"Why they got'em in there?"

"First degree murder. He's serving a twenty-five to life sentence, but I'm going to get him off. He didn't kill that woman."

Blyss had heard enough and saw how invested Beautii was into her father's case. The pain that echoed in Beautii's voice was enough to compel him to help her. "Let me see his case file. I got about an hour before it's time for me to head to court."

"Seriously?" Beautii's eyes widened in disbelief, her astonishment palpable. She couldn't wrap her mind around the fact that he was stepping up to assist her with something as raw and personal as this.

"We a team, Ms. Hamilton. We work together. We don't take no losses 'round here." Blys flashed her a confident smirk. "Let's unravel this case piece by piece. If we run into something that's out of our jurisdiction, I got connections all over the world."

"Thank you, Mr. Valentino." Beautii voiced with a smile.

"Mhm," he winked, then licked his sexy, skin toned lips. "Lead the way."

Snatching her gaze from his, Beautii led the way to the elevator. "Let's go."

As they made their way to Beautii's office, she silently thanked the Most High for aligning her with one of West Coast's most powerful, heavy hitting attorney's. Stepping into the elevator with Blyss by her side, a soft grin played at the corners of her lips as memories of her father flooded her mind. Despite his confinement behind bars, he'd still managed to be her rock, guiding her as she transitioned from a law student to a lawyer at a Tier-1 law firm. His devout support and wise advice had molded her into the powerful woman she now stood as.

"What scent do you have lingering in here?" Blyss asked as soon as he walked into Beautii's office.

Beautii laughed. "Oh, this is a *Diptyque Black Forest* soy candle by Archipelago. I ordered it from Amazon the other day," She said, reaching into her closet near her desk. "Here, you want one for your office?" Beautii offered, handing him a brand new candle. "I'ma candle fanatic, so I have plenty. This one has a more masculine scent to it, I'm sure you'll like it a lot more."

Blyss nodded his head. "Good lookin' out."

"Always," she assured him. "And, here's my father's case file. I've been studying his case for a long time, but there's still so much going on that doesn't add up." Beautii honestly admitted, handing Blyss the file.

Not a word passed between them as Blyss smoothly scanned, and flipped through the folder with a keen eye. Across the desk, Beautii watched in silence as he methodically laid out the papers before them.

"I know a PI (private investigator) and a forensic examiner who owes me a favor. Mind if I put them to work, let'em take a closer look at some of this for us?"

"God no, I don't mind. I appreciate the assist. Thank you again."

"No thanks necessary. This is what I'm about. Ain't no trouble."

There was nothing like a smooth-talking man that was not only true to his word, but true to his purpose. Blyss Valentino was the epitome of the saying, "Don't tiptoe through life, make a muthafuckas' feel every step you take. There were few in the world that were cut from the same cloth he was bred from, and Beautii was grateful to be on his team. *Fine ass man with a slick ass mouth. Jesus help ya daughter.*

---

**One Month Later…**

Groove City was known to have perfect weather everyday. It was California's sweet-spot, never scorching hot or bone-chilling cold, drawing folks from every corner of the globe to experience its splendor. From the mesmerizing blue waters that stretched out endlessly to the horizon, to the sleek yachts slicing through the waves with effortless grace, Groove City was the epitome of luxury and allure. Its skyline was adorned with opulent five-star hotels and dining establishments, each renowned for their exquisite cuisine and unparalleled service; while its neighborhoods showcased some of the most jaw-dropping homes on the planet. In the elite circles, it was a well-known fact: Groove City ranked among the top three most coveted destinations for those seeking the pinnacle of luxury living.

It was a quarter til two on a Wednesday afternoon, and the sun beat down mercilessly as Beautii and Blyss strode into the courthouse, their steps echoing confidence and determination with each step they took through the court house. This wasn't just an ordinary day; it was the first trial hearing for their client, Steven Thomas. As they entered the courtroom, the air crackled with tension, charged with the weight of impending revelations.

Judge Davis presided over the chamber, his presence

commanding respect. On one side sat the state's attorney, a formidable adversary in the legal arena. Across from him, Blyss exuded power, strength, and confidence as he was prepared to defend his client.

The proceedings began with the usual formalities, the court stenographer poised to capture every spoken word. Then came the moment of truth, the exchange of evidence, a crucial step in the legal process. Beautii listened intently, her mind racing as she took note of every detail.

"Who will be presenting first?" Judge Davis inquired, his demeanor neutral and relaxed.

"Good afternoon, your honor. I'll be presenting the state's evidence today against Steven Thomas." The state's attorney responded respectfully, leading the charge, unveiling their evidence concerning the case.

"Proceed," Judge Davis granted, signaling the start of the proceedings.

"Yes, your honor. In regards to the deaths of Tatum Edwards and Gavin Sanchez, we've uncovered two firearms and recovered fingerprints from the crime scene. Additionally, we have witnesses present today prepared to testify against Mr. Steven Thomas," the state's attorney elaborated, his words concise yet commanding.

Judge Davis scribbled some things on the paper sitting in front of him, then shifted his gaze to Blyss.

"Attorney Valentino, good afternoon." Judge Davis greeted with a nod. "Proceed.

"Good afternoon, your honor, It's always a pleasure." Blyss returned the greeting, his tone smooth and confident. "At this time I'd like to present video footage from Edwin Moore and Jackie Adams' *Ring* doorbell. The whole incident was captured. Furthermore, I have DNA evidence, thoroughly tested and conclusively not matching my client.

Blyss rose to his feet, a master conductor orchestrating the symphony of their defense. With precision, he laid out their strategy, each word calculated to undermine the prosecution's case. Then, like a well-timed revelation, he revealed their ace in the hole—the camera footage. As the footage played, time seemed to stand still in the courtroom. Every eye was glued to the screen, the truth unfolding before them like a movie. Doubts surfaced, casting shadows over the prosecution's claims, and exposing cracks in their narrative; which ultimately turned the tide in their favor.

Judge Davis observed silently, his expression unreadable as he absorbed the information before him.

"With all that was presented today, it's my decision to reconvene in two weeks." Judge Davis concluded, his voice carrying the weight of authority.

"I appreciate everything you doin' to get me back out there with my family." Steven Thomas told Blyss before being escorted out by correctional officers.

"It's all good. You'll be hearing from me again soon." Blyss quickly assured his client.

With the hearing adjourned, Beautii and Blyss shared a knowing glance, a silent vow to keep fighting. As they stepped out into the harsh light of day, they carried with them a newfound sense of purpose. For in the relentless pursuit of truth, they were a force to be reckoned with. And with their client's fate hanging in the balance, they were prepared to unleash hell to uncover the truth.

"You really held it down in there," Beautii complimented Blyss as they walked out of the courtroom.

"That was light work," Blyss dismissed. "They still gon' try to pin that shit on him, but ain't nothin' they gon' be able to do once they find out what else is up our sleeve. Were you able to speak to any of the witnesses?"

"Only one of them so far, but I'll be reaching out to the others again when we get back to the office."

"Let's stop and get somethin' to eat first, then we can swing by their houses afterwards. You cool wit' that?"

"Yes! I am starving. I didn't eat anything for breakfast this morning."

Blyss chuckled. "I got the perfect spot in mind," Blyss told her as he unlocked his car door from his key fob. "I hope you like tacos."

---

As soon as Beautii stepped through the threshold of her home, a wave of peace and tranquility washed over her. The familiar scent of cleanliness and the gentle aroma of her favorite plug-in awakened her senses, instantly putting her at ease. The soft murmur of the wind filtering through the cracked window, carried with it a whisper of nature's serenade.

Her gaze is inevitably drawn to the sun setting beyond the horizon, giving off a soft radiance through the blinds, and sheer white curtains that sway gently in the breeze. The interplay of light and shadow created a mesmerizing dance, infusing her living space with a palette of golden hues and amber tones.

As she stood by the window, entranced by the beauty of the scene before her, her mind began to wander. Memories and thoughts drifted like clouds across the canvas of her consciousness, each one carrying its own weight and significance. In this moment of quiet reflection, amidst the soothing embrace of what Beautii called her sweet spot; she found herself pondering the journey that had brought her to a bittersweet current reality.

Balance.

Time.

Clarity.

If there was one thing in the world Beautii despised more than anything, it was instability. Every goal she had set for herself had been accomplished, everything she had prayed for was coming together, and she was seeing more good than bad days. However, there was one man alone responsible for the pain she undoubtedly felt in her heart. It felt like a sneak attack because it had hit her so unexpectedly. She never saw herself being the kind of woman who held on mentally and emotionally to a man who meant her no good, and harmful to her soul in ways she couldn't explain.

As she stood in the window reflecting on the time she and Bilaal spent together, she'd be a liar if she said she didn't miss him. The truth was, she longed for him in the worst way, but even that wasn't enough to make her back pedal into a situationship that would land her in the same place she was fighting to free her father from. She was indeed tossed between two opinions, and the instability she felt as she warred within herself had her anxiety rising to insane levels. Beautii was at the inception of her personal inner healing, soul examination journey; even though it didn't feel good right now, she knew it was necessary for her to experience the pain so she could appreciate her wholeness.

The rumbling of her stomach quickly brought her back down to earth, reminding her that she hadn't eaten all day long. Exhaling a deep sigh, she made her way to the kitchen, grateful for her prior preparation of meals for the week. With hands freshly washed, the salmon salad she had waiting for her in the refrigerator called her name. After plating her food with care, its savory aroma made her mouth water as she poured herself a generous glass of red wine, then settled into a stool at the island.

Beautii had a lot to unpack and put into perspective, and the truth of the matter is that very little had to do with Bilaal. The journey to healing she was on had everything to do with putting herself first, understanding her worth, and rediscovering herself on a level that aligned with where her hard work, diligence, and focus had manifested for her. In this case time was on her side, because there was nothing, or no one worth rushing her process for. Life had taught her that whatever's meant for her will find its way to her, the only job she had was to make sure she was ready to receive.

## CHAPTER FOUR

### BEAUTII HAMILTON

*Two Years Later...*

*Spotless Mind* by Jhene Aiko streamed easily through the speakers of Beautii's brand new black 2023 Mercedes-Benz S580, as she cruised down the expressway. After working diligently on her father's case, she'd finally found a loophole significant enough to guarantee his release from prison. Bruce had served seven years as an innocent man in prison, and out of all the times Beautti traveled this same road to visit him; she was filled with pure joy because finally she had good news to tell him. Blyss had even pulled a few strings to help Beautii get connected with top tier investigators, and a few agents he was connected with to gather further information. Now that Beautii lived in the heart of Groove City, what used to be a three hour drive; now only took forty-five minutes.

 Beautii loved everything about being a lawyer. Her life was still a bit stressful, but it was a different kind of stress. It was one thing to struggle financially, put up with a man that didn't love you right, and graduate early and at the top of your law class. This was the type of stress she could completely live without, and was glad she no longer had to deal with it. Beautii had grown accustomed to waking up early, staying up late working on cases. Everyday she learned new strategies, and sides of the law she never would have been able to experience if it wasn't for Blyss. If there was one thing Beautii could change about her life, she wouldn't change one thing. Her success was in the palm of her hands, and she owed every blessing to date to God, and Blyss Valentino.

Pulling into the parking lot of Groove City Prison, Beautii grabbed the black folder from the passenger seat, killed her engine, then made her way to the intake lobby to be processed in the facility.

"Good morning," Beautii politely stated. "I'm here to see Bruce Hamilton. I'm his attorney."

"Good morning, just a second," the correctional officer replied, as he handed another officer a key. "I'll need to see your license and bar card please."

"Oh you do have manners," a man sitting in the far right of the lobby interrupted. "You've been talking to all of us like shit, but now you wanna be nice 'cause this fine ass lawyer walked in here. On me, this nigga full of shit." He gripped and shook his head in disgust.

"Forgive us for the disruption, these are the typical things we have to deal with daily." The officer explained, unaware of the guilty expression displayed on his face. "Everything checks out. You can follow Officer Slacum after you walk through the metal detector."

"Thank you," Beautii replied, after getting a good look at the officer's name plate.

"Your visit has been terminated. You'll get a letter in the

OASIS

mail in two or three weeks telling you why, and when you can come back for another visit." The officer told the man who pulled his card.

"My visit is terminated for what? I ain't do shit."

"You can leave peacefully, or you can be detained. Your choice." The officer cut him off, ready to follow through with the latter end of his statement.

"This is bullshit and you know it man. We come here to see our people, we deserve some respect. We not the fucking criminals!" The man based before storming out of the prison pissed.

Beautii knew how to mind her business, but the lawyer in her couldn't stand injustice. It had already settled in her mind to report the officer once she finished visiting with her father. She could only imagine how the officers were treating her father, if they were mistreating visitors like this. She couldn't help but look around at every single detail of the prison. For the life of her, she didn't know how her father lived under such conditions. One thing was certain, and two things for sure; she honored and respected him more because of it. Prison has a way of humbling a person, and the fact that her father remained a man through the process spoke volumes of his character.

"You can come right through these doors. Mr. Hamilton will be down shortly to meet with you," Officer Slacum told Beautii before turning around and closing the door behind him.

The faint sound of Bruce's laughter let Beautii know her father wasn't far away. Seconds later, Bruce entered the room, and Beautii stood to her feet and waited for Officer Slacum to uncuff her father.

"Whenever you're ready to leave, I'll be close by. Just

43

knock on the door," Officer Slacum announced, then turned around and secured the door behind him.

"Attorney Beautii Hamilton," Bruce was in awe of his daughter. "Look at you. Come give your old man some love." He opened his arms to embrace his daughter. "It's so good to see you."

"I'm glad to see you too, dad. You haven't aged one bit," Beautii complimented her father's timeless features. "How's everything going in here? I know it's not perfect, due to the circumstances; I'm makin' out alright. How are you really doing?"

"One day at a time, Beautii," Bruce told her genuinely. "I loathe waking up in this hell hole everyday, but I gotta do what I gotta do. In my mind, I was only locked up for about three months."

"Three months? You've been here for seven years."

"It took me three months to adjust. Three months to learn my way around, and observe everything that goes on in here. From that day forward, I accepted these conditions and became content."

"How?"

"I'm an innocent man, Beautii. I'm not serving a life sentence, I'm serving a purpose."

"What purpose are you serving behind bars?" In Beautii's mind, there was no purpose more important than her father being present in her and her mother's life.

"Since I've been away, I've been able to do a lot of work on myself. In the process of building myself up more, I've been able to inspire younger men that got themselves caught up," Bruce explained. "I've seen a lot in my life, and it's been a blessing and a curse being locked down in here. Make no mistake, your daddy is ready to come home. I hate that I've had to miss one second away from you or your mother."

"I got some good news for you," Beautii smiled, and shifted the conversation. She loved her daddy something serious, it didn't take much to bring her to tears.

"Oh yeah? Let's hear it." Bruce sat attentively, with his hands clasped together with pure anticipation of Beautii's next words.

"Blyss and I finally have enough evidence to prove your innocence." Beautii happily revealed with a smile.

Bruce let out a deep sigh of relief, as a single tear fell from the brim of his eye. "Thank you."

"Here's the paperwork that breaks everything down for you. We just got approved to get back in court in two months." Beautii revealed, as her father looked over the papers.

"This is some real good news, Beautii. I appreciate everything you've been doing for me. I really do. You and your mother are my constant reason for holding on until brighter days come." Bruce said, as he scanned over the legal documents with a smile on his face.

"I haven't told mom about this yet. I wanted you to be the first to know."

"Yea, let's keep it between us. I don't wanna subject her to anymore of this bullshit. Once I'm free, I wanna surprise her in a special way," Bruce nodded. "I love and miss her more than she'll ever know."

"She misses you like crazy too, daddy. I can't wait for both of you to start living again. You know, like… the way you were before all this travesty occurred." Beautii sighed deeply.

Bruce did a good job of concealing his true feelings behind the facade of being alright behind bars. The truth was that everyday behind bars was hell on earth, but he'd never work Beautii's nerves up by telling her his raw truth. While Bruce had the opportunity to leave a lasting impression on a lot of men's lives in a positive way, he was doing all he could to survive behind bars everyday. Majority of the deaths, sicknesses, pregnancies, cruel and unusual punishment that took place in prison never made it to the news or the newspaper. Men had their manhood taken away everyday behind bars, and there were more fiend's than a little bit. Contrary to popular belief, everything that was available on the street was accessible in prison. Bruce stayed away from drugs and gangs while doing his time. He didn't want anything standing in his way when it was time for him to be released from that hell hole.

"It's gonna be just like I never left when I get home, just watch and see.

"I hate to cut our time short. I have to make it back in time to sit in on this other case I've been working on with Blyss," Beautii sadly revealed. Walking away was always the hardest part for both of them. The only thing that made it easier was knowing that time was winding down.

"I love you, Beautii. Keep on doing what you're doing," Bruce stood up and opened his arms wide to embrace his daughter.

"I love you too, daddy," Beautii walked into her father's warm embrace and squeezed tightly. "I'll see you soon," Beautii kissed his jaw, then tapped on the door so the guard could let her and her father out.

Standing at the door while the officer's reshackled his wrists, Bruce watched his daughter walk away until he could no longer see her anymore. Beautii and her mother were his entire heart. Nothing else in the world mattered to him if he didn't have them.

*Two Months Later...*

Sitting at the breakfast nook drinking a hot cup of tea, and observing the entrancing oasis outside of the window; Beautii gathered her thoughts. The day she'd been patiently waiting for, and working overtime to prepare for had finally arrived. Beautii was a lawyer and she wanted to have faith in the system, she understood justice was often an afterthought for those with melanated skin tones. *Trust me Beautii, I don't sell dreams. I serve realities. Your father is coming home tomorrow.* Blyss' words replayed in her mind a million times. Out of all the facts she'd gathered for her father's case, the only thing that gave her peace was the assurance of Blyss' words. He managed to eradicate every ounce of uneasiness that laid dormant in her mind and heart. The fact still remained since she'd been working with him; he'd never lost a case.

"Lord, please work it out for us. Let your will be done." Beautii whispered a solemn prayer, then drank the rest of her tea. It was four o'clock in the morning, yet Beautii was sending up her petitions, and commanding her day. Getting up from her seat, Beautii pushed her chair in, then quickly washed her cup, and placed it in the dish rack. Once she ascended the stairs, she went straight to her walk-in closet that was attached to her master bedroom. She decided on a navy blue pencil skirt suit, ivory colored camisole, paired with a nude designer heels.

Beautii continued her morning routine as her mind raced a million different directions. Her photographic memory was in full affect, as she mentally went over the evidence of her fathers case. She found herself getting upset every time she thought about it. Grabbing a fresh fluffy towel and two face cloths from the linen closet, Beautii reached down and turned on the hot water as high as she could stand it. As the ariel bathtub filled with water, she dropped some Miss Dior bath bombs in the water, then stood in front of the sink and washed her face and brushed her teeth.

An hour and a half later, Beautii stood in front of her floor to ceiling mirror fully dressed, makeup beat to the gods', and combed down her wrap. The sound of her phone ringing and vibrating against her nightstand caught her attention over the peaceful nature sounds that she kept playing in her room at all times.

"Hello, this is Beautii," she answered sweetly, placing the call on speaker, so she could continue to comb her hair.

"Good morning, Beautii. How are you?" Jillian the front desk clerk and office paralegal asked. "I was just calling to check on you. I know this is your big day." After working together for the last two years, Jillian and Beautii had become really good friends. Even Fayth loved her.

"Yes! I am beyond ready for all of this to be over. I can't wait to see the look on my mom's face when we surprise her." Beautii grabbed her bottle of *Miss Dior,* and sprayed herself all over with it.

"Alright lady. Bliss is headed downtown now to meet you. He just left," Jillian told Beautii.

"Okay, well let me go so I can make it there on time. Keep your fingers crossed for us."

"Chille, it's already done. I'll talk to you later."

Beautii concluded the call, then grabbed her navy blue and gold Louis Vuiton bag. After turning off the lights in her room, she descended the stairs at seven-thirty sharp. Leaving her exactly one hour to make it to the court house. After setting her house alarm, she quickly grabbed her keys off the key ring right beside her front door, then secured her locks.

*One Hour Later…*

"Good morning, thank you for coming to show your support. I truly appreciate all you've done to assist me in my fathers case," Beautii told Blyss as soon as she made it to the front of the courtroom.

"Don't shortcut yourself. Most of this is all your work, I just filled in a few blanks. It was no problem at all. I take care of my team," Blyss winked his eye and replied. Soon after their greeting, two of Groove City's correctional officers escorted Beautii's father into the courtroom. Stylishly adorned in an all black Tom Ford suit, black loafers, and a fresh cut; Bruce Hamilton entered the courtroom looking like new money. It was a light embellishment from Blyss. His sole intentions were to present Bruce in the best light possible, therefore, wearing prison blues' wasn't an option. Besides the look on Beautii's face was payment enough. Beautii and Blyss had the opportunity to partner in a lot of cases together during the two years they'd been working together. Blyss was more than confident in Beautii's ability to take on this case without him. However, he was there just in case the state attorney tried to throw a curveball.

"Wish us luck," Beautii sighed deeply, and told Blyss.

"You don't need luck when you have me on your team," Blyss confidently replied.

Bruce had been in prison serving a twenty-five years to life sentence for a murder he didn't commit. He'd been wrongfully identified in a line up by a traumatized white woman for killing her sister. Bruce had a reputation of violence, and had even been hemmed up a few times for assault in his younger years. However, he'd managed to get out of the game before local law enforcement got a chance to snatch his life away from him. For years they tried to take him down, but he'd humiliated the system, and made a clear exit from the game before they were able to hang him out to dry for good. Beautii was the deciding factor that changed his life for the better. He made a vow to God, his wife, and Beautii that he'd never revert back into his old ways. Becoming a father was the best thing that ever happened to him.

"Hey daddy, you look good. Where did you get these clothes from?" Beautii quizzed, then followed the direction of her father's eyes as he looked back at Blyss and nodded his head.

"All rise," the bailiff announced as Judge Wilson made his entrance into the courtroom. Once he took his seat, everyone else followed suit. "Today we'll be hearing case #XSf893579461, Bruce Hamilton." The judge announced, then spoke a few other words to the stenographer to write for the record, before getting started with the hearing.

"Who will be representing Bruce Hamilton today with his appeal?" Judge Wilson asked.

"I will Your Honor," Beautii stood and spoke up clearly.

"Please state your name for the record."

"Attorney Beautii Hamilton."

"My record is showing that there's some new evidence found concerning the case that's in need of review. If you're ready, you may present it at this time." Judge Wilson announced, and gestured with his head.

"Before getting started with the factual evidence I have on paper, I'd like to play a recording that the state's prosecutor failed to present during the initial court hearing eight years ago." Beautii said, then pressed play.

"Mrs. Baker I know you're upset, but I need you to work with me. Help me help you." Detective Spriggs pleaded.

"I don't know what else you want me to say," Mrs Baker cried. "I told you it was dark, and I couldn't make out the man's face. All I saw was a lion tattoo on his neck. He appeared to be light skinned." Mrs. Baker yelled. "You keep trying to pull information out of me, and I keep telling you I don't remember much outside of what I've already told you. We were on our way out to get a few drinks like we always did on a Saturday night. We made it to the car, and as soon as we reached forward to open the door, we were attacked." Mrs. Baker explained. "There was a man strangling me from behind, demanding that I give them my purse and the keys to my car. I obeyed, but my sister refused. She attempted to fight back, and her neck was slit immediately after. This is all I can remember before I was knocked unconscious."

"Look at these pictures Mrs. Baker. Take a close look at these pictures, and tell me which one of these men killed your sister. Is this him?" Detective Spriggs badgered, then held up the picture and asked. "That's all you have to do is tell me it was him, and I'll make sure his ass never see's the light of day again. For God sake! Get justice for your sister!"

"Yes!" Mrs. Baker lied, then broke down and cried harder. "Yes! That's him! All black people look alike anyway."

"Very good, Mrs. Baker. Now we're getting somewhere. You've done well," Detective Spriggs encouraged, then deviously snickered.

Beautti stopped the recording, then looked up at Judge Wilson. "What I've just played for you is a live recording of Detective Spriggs badgering the victim, and the witness who's statement was used in sentencing Mr. Hamilton. In addition, I'd also like to point out how the statement of Mrs. Baker changed not once, not twice, but three times during the investigation. When our private investigator went to see her, she admitted that her statement was coerced. She also stated that Detective Spriggs threatened her several times, telling her that if she ever breathed one word of the truth; he'd kill her and her family." Beautii revealed and passed Judge Wilson a copy of all three written statements, and a fourth that was written telling the truth about what she really saw. Nothing. "I am requesting that my client be released immediately. Clearly he's been serving time for a crime he didn't commit, Your Honor."

Judge Wilson reviewed the statements, then looked up and noticed Detective Spriggs trying to slip out of court without being seen. "Cuff him, and bring him to me." Judge Wilson ordered the officers of the court. "I'm disgusted with what I've heard here today. Detective Spriggs you are being charged with perjury, coercion, and for threatening a victim. There will be no bail! Get him out of my courtroom." Judge Wilson infuriated, as he was an African American judge himself, who actually had a heart. "Mr. Hamilton, a simple apology isn't enough. The system did you an enormous disservice, and the time subtracted from your life can never be replenished. My just ruling today is time served. Mr. Hamilton you are free to go home with your family today," Judge Wilson said. "Uncuff this innocent man. Court is adjourned." Judge Wilson banged his gavel, then got up to leave.

Instant memories flashed, and all the hard work that had been invested in Bruce's case had finally paid off. Beautii undoubtedly transformed from a lawyer to a daughter who missed her daddy terribly. Once her father was unshackled, Beautii ran, and leaped into her father's arms; like a toddler being reunited with her parents.

"Thank you Jesus," Bruce closed his eyes and

acknowledged his creator. Truly, He'd proven to be a righteous judge.

"Daddy! I've missed you so much." Beautii cried and held her father tight.

Blyss stood back and witnessed the miracle of grace in unadulterated form. Everyone who was present in the courtroom had cleared out by the time Beautii and her father let each other go, except Blyss.

"Blyss Valentino," Bruce called. "There's no way I can repay you and my daughter for what y'all have done for me. Thank you." Bruce said genuinely, as he walked in Blyss' direction.

"This is the reason I became a lawyer," Blyss revealed. "Freedom is something that's predestined for all of us. I was just a vehicle that helped speed up the process. Timing is everything in this life," Blyss assessed.

"You're a wise man. We gotta get together real soon," Bruce said. "I like this suit too, man. Got an old man feeling young again."

"You know we couldn't have you out here any kinda way," Blyss added.

"Well, let's go get something to eat. I know you're ready to eat some real food right about now, huh?" Beautii chimed in with a smile.

"Yes, Lawd," Bruce agreed.

※

Future's *You Deserve It,* oozed moderately through Blyss' car speakers as he pulled up to a restaurant called Langston & Suks. Instinctively, Bruce and Blyss scanned the atmosphere. It was an innate trait that all protective and territorial men did anytime they went to a place that they would be subjected to the energy, attitudes, and other unforeseen situations. Both Blyss and Bruce were Alpha's and they didn't play about the leading ladies in their life, or those around them who were of significant value.

"Wow," Bruce said, as his lips mildly trembled, and a few tears fell from his eyes. Serving eight years in prison had changed him. Humbled him. He appreciated the simple things in life. Blyss and Beautii; however, had outdone themselves. Langston & Suks was beyond extravagant. Excitement. Genuine happiness. Appreciation. At once, Bruce felt each emotion so deeply they manifested through his tears. "Damn, all this for an old man?"

"You deserve this and so much more, daddy. This is just the beginning," Beautii spoke from the heart, and matched his tears with a free flow of her own. Patiently, Blyss stood back and allowed Beautii and her father to have their moment. It was admirable how much they loved each other. Their connection was so pure. "Come on, daddy. Let's go get some barbeque," Beautii insisted, knowing that Bruce loved himself some good barbeque ribs. "You ready," she asked Blyss, while intertwining her fingers with her father's.

Langston & Suks was a very upscale restaurant that countless celebrities frequented, among other high-class, cultured people who loved the dual fine dining experience. Not to mention the broad lounge section. Blyss introduced Beautii to it about a year prior, when he and Jillian took her out to eat for her birthday. Langston & Suks specialized in every fine dining cuisine, including nouvelle cuisine, and other haute dishes people traveled the world to experience. As they stepped inside the restaurant, they were met by a very friendly host.

"Good afternoon. My name is Monica," the host

introduced herself. "Do you have a reservation?" She asked politely, before grabbing the menus that sat on the podium.

"Good afternoon, Monica," Beautii replied. "We have a section reserved under Hamilton."

"Oh okay. Yes ma'am, follow me right this way," Monica led the way to their section with a smile.

The savory smell of soul food wafted through the air, and into their nostrils; like a smooth breeze over the ocean. A few feet away from their designated section, Bruce and Mea's eyes connected. Time stood still, voices ceased, and everyone around them froze in place. For eight years, Mea had grieved the loss of her husband, and longed to be with him again. She experienced major depression, and put herself through isolation periods, where she refused to communicate with anyone. Beautii and her best friend Fayth had to put their minds together to figure out how to get Mea out of the house. Although they had to mildly bend the truth, they figured it would be all worth it at the end. And, it was when they got to witness the reuniting of two souls right in front of their eyes. They were one of love's truest representatives in Beautii's eyes.

Bruce and Mea took slow, weighted steps towards each other; hearts pounding in their chest; as they anticipated each other's touch. Reaching up to caress the sides of her husbands' face, tears flowed from her eyes; and prickled in his.

"Bruce," Mea whispered, then wrapped her arms around him tightly.

"Mea, baby," Bruce replied. "I've waited so long for this moment."

"It's perfect. I've missed you so much." Mea cried tears of joy, as she rubbed up and down his back.

*"Oh, I've been thinkin' of you, and you've been thinkin' of me. Oh, I'll give all that I have. If you'll give all that I need . And, oh, let's be fair. And, I think it's time we cleared the air. You've been watchin' me, I've been watchin' you. You know I've been wanting to groove with you…"*

Bruce whispered the words to the Isley Brothers *Groove With You* directly in her ear, causing her to swoon under his touch. Ever since they spent their first Valentine's Day together in high school, the Isley Brothers played such a major part in knitting their hearts together with love. This was the theme song that played in the background the night Beautii was conceived. Bruce was smooth back in the day, and nothing at all had changed. His voice. His charisma. His dominance. Mea's heart melted at the feel of his rhythmically against her chest.

"I love you, and I've missed you too." Bruce told her genuinely, then kissed her passionately.

"Ehm," Beautii interrupted their moment. "Can y'all finish this up later? Like when y'all get to the hotel.

"You too old to still be blockin' Beautii," Blyss joked, causing Mea and Bruce to laugh.

The love and excitement was so potent, everyone watching couldn't help but feel, appreciate, respect, and be inspired by it.

"Hey sis!" Fayth excitedly greeted.

"Hey sis!" Beautii returned excitedly. "Thank you for being here with me for this. I couldn't have pulled this off without you.

"Y'all lil heffa's tricked me good," Beautii's mom replied, nodding her head. "This is the best surprise I could ever receive. Thank you so much.

"You're welcome, mommy. The reward of your smile made all of this well worth it." Beautii replied, honestly.

"Hello everyone, my name is Laniyah. I'll be your server today, can I get you all started with some drinks?" She asked politely.

"Yes! I'll take an apple martini, and a strawberry lemonade please." Fayth requested, then continued to look over the menu.

"I'll have the same," Beautii said, aiming her phone over the barcode so she could review the menu as well.

"I'll have a glass of red wine please," Beautii's mom ordered.

"She'll have a glass of the best red wine you have to offer," Bruce wrapped his arm around his wife's shoulder and requested.

"And, my husband here will have a long island iced tea, extra liquor." Mea looked over and winked at Bruce. The instant glow that appeared on her face was impossible not to notice. Blyss was very observant, and was completely amazed because it wasn't sex infused. If Monica's song *Love All Over Me* had a face, it would be Mea and Bruce.

Inwardly, Beautii craved the kind of love her parents shared. Easy flowing and transparent. Natural and satisfying. Real love was a high commodity, but seeing her parents together again brought everything back into perspective.

"I'll have a vodka martini," Blyss ordered, then looked over his menu.

"Coming right up," Laniyah replied before she turned to walk away.

Langston & Suks was the kind of restaurant that gave all the feels. Though it was mid-day, the vibe was so smooth and intimate; the dim lighting made it feel so cozy, it didn't matter.

"I think I want some fried catfish today, with some cheesy grits and shrimp," Beautii announced. "Oh and a house salad." Beautii closed her menu and looked at her friend Fayth. "What you getting, girly?"

"Umm, I think I want some steak, and loaded garlic mashed potatoes," Fayth answered.

"What about you, Blyss?" Beautii Inquired.

"I think I'ma get this glazed salmon, cajun rice with shrimp, and cabbage." Blyss closed his menu and said.

"Umm, that sounds good," Beautii licked her lips. "What about you two love birds?" Beautii made reference to her parents.

"You already know I'm getting this rack of barbecue ribs, mac-n-cheese, and greens. Oh yeah, and I want some sweet potatoes too," Bruce said.

"I think I want a seafood boil," Mea said as Laniyah walked back to the table and passed out everyone's drinks.

Once Laniyah wrote everyone's food order down, she disappeared again afterwards, so she could put it in promptly.

## CHAPTER FIVE

### BILAAL HARRIS

Sitting on the opposite side of the restaurant, Bilaal struggled to steady the cluster of emotions that spun out of control inside his mind, heart, and in the pit of his stomach. He'd gone two long years without seeing Beautii, and swore to himself that if he ever saw her again, he'd make things right with her. At the time when he and Beautii entered each other's lives, Bilaal was knee deep in the game. His last concern was being the man he knew Beautii needed. Bilaal came from the trenches, but was well aware of what it truly took to be the man he needed to be. However, he was too selfish to see beyond his own desires. Beautii was everything a man could ever ask for in a woman. Smart. Goal oriented. Genuine. Sexy. Those were just a few things Bilaal loved about Beautii.

Secretly, he'd prayed for God to grant him one wish; to lay eyes on the love of his life one more time. He felt like all he needed was one more shot to get in Beautii's good graces, and the rest would be history. Bilaal was the epitome of a man with big dreams, no heart, and no real character. He thought his money was the answer to all his problems, and for so long it was. His money had bought him everything he could possibly need, and he had no wants; except for Beautii.

When he'd met Beautii, she didn't have much materialistically, but she was the wealthiest woman Bilaal had ever been in the presence of. Her soul, her mind, her heart, and her value far exceeded any woman he'd ever been with. He thought that she'd never be strong enough to leave him, but she had, and never looked back once since she left. Bilaal regretted the day he'd turned his back on her. His entitlement and arrogance wouldn't allow him to apologize, or beg her to stay with him. Living with regrets had been a reality check like no other. Urgent desperation bolted through his body at lightning speed the longer he sat across the room, and watched Beautii entertain her people.

"Ehm," Willow cleared her throat. "What are you looking at? I'm over here." Willow said seductively, trying to regain Bilaal's attention. Agitated, she followed his line of sight, then sighed deeply, as both recognition and defeat spread across her innocent face. She knew exactly who Beautii was, and blessed the day she left Bilaal. She loathed the fact that once again, Bilaal was gawking over a woman who was above his and her caliber. "Are you serious, Bilaal?" Willow smacked her lips, and rolled her eyes hard. "I've been begging you to bring me here for a whole year, and now you can't even finish our conversation?" Her voice cracked. "You promised things were going to be different, but all this is the same shit in reverse."

With his hand, Bilaal shooed Willow dismissively, and right before her eyes, Bilaal zeroed in on Beautii. Willow was so distraught, she was speechless. She was pregnant with her second child, and still, Bilaal refused to give her the commitment she deserved. Willow had a hard head, and her heart consistently created disasters she struggled to digest. Every woman should know a baby won't keep a man, no matter how many you have. Willow had given Bilaal her all, and for so long, she settled for mere scraps. She wanted more. She deserved more, but was running out of ideas.

Lil Baby's *California Breeze* spilled loudly from the speakers, and Bilaal sat back nodding his head in deep thought concerning his next move. Across the restaurant's dining room, Beautii and her family finished eating, and were sitting around the table laughing and enjoying each other's company.

"Come on y'all, this is my song. Let's dance," Fayth insisted, as she rose from her seat, pushing her chair up to the table. Everyone got up and followed fayth to the dance floor. Fayth was a free spirit as she danced alone, feeling the beat. Bruce and Mea grooved together the same as they'd done since they were younger. While Beautii and Blyss surrendered to the natural, magnetic pull that drew them together. Turning around, Beautii swayed her hips, and lightly twirled her ass against Blyss' manhood. Grabbing her waist, he rode the beat, and rhythmically kept up with Beautii's movements.

Green with envy, the effects of jealousy ate away at Bilaal's heart like a cancer. Seeing Beautii dancing with another man sickened him, and caused him to see nothing but red. *Not my baby.* Bilaal couldn't believe Beautii had moved on already. He couldn't pinpoint if the reality of her moving on with another man, or seeing another man give her what he couldn't was worse. Either way, his territorial nature had gotten the best of him, and he could no longer sit still.

"I'll be back, Willow," Bilaal told her, then slipped out of his seat, and made his way to Beautii. Bilaal could care less about timing, all he wanted was to be back in Beautii's life. From the pictures he'd seen in the past, he knew her parents were there, and he recognized Fayth from the few times she'd stopped by the house when he was home. Still, Bilaal didn't give a damn, simply put.

"Aye', let me holla at you real quick," Bilaal demanded with the look of death present in his eyes.

The shock written all over Beautii's face was impossible to hide. "Excuse me?" Beautii squinted her eyes, and stepped back further into Blyss' strong arms; as if he was her covering. "What are you doing here?" Beautii asked, taken aback by his presence.

"Look, I know it's been a while, but all a nigga tryna do is holla at chu' for a minute. Can I do that?" Bilaal said, still refusing to take his eyes off of Blyss.

"Beautii, you want me to handle this for you?" Blyss offered, protectively wrapping his arm around Beautii's waist, pulling her close; forgetting about all he stood to lose. He didn't take disrespect lightly. Blyss had made it out of the trenches, but it didn't take much for him to remember his roots. Beautii's hesitation to speak alarmed him. "Say bruh, this ain't the time or the place. If you got some business with Beautii, call her later." Blyss advised a lot milder than he wanted to out of respect for Beautii's parents being in close proximity..

Blyss was known to be a man of prominence. He didn't lower his standard to entertain matters that were beneath him. However, the script had easily been flipped when it came to Beautii Hamilton. There was something majestic about her that Blyss had noticed the day she walked into his office. Patiently, he tried to identify her superpower, but everytime he thought he was close; he became mesmerized all over again. Beyond her exquisite beauty, her smooth, melanated, gingerbread complexion. Her naturally long hair, and tawny colored eyes held the perfect dual combination of purity and seduction. Blyss was a protector, and he had the heart of a warrior. They'd been dancing less than five minutes, and Blyss had already found himself stuck in her trance. He didn't know the nature of Bilaal and Beautii's relationship, but one thing was certain; they'd see each other again. It was only a matter of time.

"Yo, fuck all'lat-"

"We got a problem over here?" Bruce asked Blyss, but kept his eyes on Bilaal. He'd just gotten released from prison, but he'd go back in the blink of an eye for his baby girl. This time, he'd be found guilty as charged.

"It's nice to meet you, Mr. Hamilton," Bilaal pretentiously stated.

"Beautii, what's going on here?" Mea asked, confused by the shift in everybodies energy all of a sudden.

"You need to leave now, Bilaal," Beautii fumed, exasperated by his presence; vehemently pointing her shaky finger in his face. "I said all I needed to say to you two years ago. That chapter of my life has been sealed."

"I know, baby, but I've changed. That's all I wanted to tell you. I'm not even tryna cause a scene. Just let me talk to you," Bilaal begged.

Beautii shook her head in disgust. "You can front all you want, but the universe responds to the real you, not who you're pretending to be." Beautii read him like a book. "From where I stand, you're still the same selfish nigga I left two years ago."

"I'm not the same man, Beautii. Just let me show you I can be better for you." Bilaal protested, and urged. Trying his best to force his way past Beautii's resistance, yet failing terribly.

"Show me better than you can tell me," Beautii challenged. "Walk away."

Bilaal's saddened eyes failed to break through Beautii's

unyielding exterior. Nodding his head, he backed away without saying another mumbling word. *This shit ain't over yet, I'll be back.*

"Let's go," Bilaal hastily told Willow.

"What? I'm not finished with my food yet," Willow smacked her lips, and continued to eat her food.

"Man, I ain't got time for this shit. Hurry up so I can drop you off. I got some other shit I need to get to." Bilaal impatiently stated. "Matter fact, here," Bilaal reached into his pocket, and tossed a stack on the table. "This should cover it, I'll be in the car when you get done." Bilaal turned to walk away, and noticed Beautii's eyes planted on him and Willow. Beautii shook her head, then turned to walk back to her table with Blyss. Bilaal knew his approach was extremely preposterous, but he needed to make his presence known; no matter how absurd his method was. Defeated. Looking towards the ground, Bilaal searched his heart for the answer to the lingering question in his mind since he'd set his eyes on Beautii again. *How can I right my wrongs?*

---

Deep. Reflective. Scattered. As Bilaal took the three hour ride back to Sacramento, his thoughts were deep, reflective, and scattered in a million different directions. The savage side of him wanted to yank Beautii up right in the middle of the dance floor. While the other side of him knew that action wouldn't fly with her father standing there. *Who the fuck was that nigga she was dancing with.* Bilaal's serious face became disconfigured the more his mind danced around the what if's.

Willow sat on the passenger side staring at him in utter disbelief. Bilaal had charmed her, deceived her, and led her on to believe they'd be a family with their two children. For the last year, Willow had witnessed significant changes within Bilaal. If not for her sake, she hoped and prayed that it would last for their children. Bilaal had developed a pattern of disappointing her through the years, but something in her gut confirmed that he was really trying to do better. Beautii had stood in the way of their happiness in the past, but since she'd been out of the picture things had been better.

Be careful what you ask for because you just might get it. If Willow would've known they were going to run into Beautii, she never would have begged Bilaal to take her to Langston & Suks. Now that she'd been granted her wish, she desperately wished she could turn back the hands of time. They'd had Tank's Sex Love & Pain album on repeat the whole way to Groove City, but when *Better For You* came on, a fresh stream of tears slid down Willow's face. Memories of her and Bilaal having make up sex to this song flooded her mind. Every time he'd fucked up, she'd forgiven him, and told herself, *he's just a man.*

"Willow," Bilaal said. Pulling into her driveway, there was a sudden uneasiness that came over her, intuition if you will. Deep down she felt like Bilaal was about to let her down again. Even her daughter felt the shift, and delivered lethal kicks as she anticipated his next words.

"Willow, I'm not tryna hurt you no more than I already have. We been on and off for a long time now, and ain't nothing gon' change between us. I'm not the man for you, and you ain't the woman I'm in love with," Bilaal broke the silence, and tried his best to explain his true feelings.

"So, that's it?" Willow cried. "You promised me that we were going to be together. We were doing fine until you saw that bitch at the restaurant! She wouldn't even give you the time of day, and she left yo' ass! But now it's fuck me, and all we've been building together for the last two years?" Willow absently caressed her belly, as she attempted to sooth her baby. "Fuck you, Bilaal!" Willow seethed. "What about our son, and our daughter that'll be coming into the world in the next few months?"

"I said I don't want to do this shit with you no more. That ain't got a damn thing to do with my seeds. I can take care of my kids, and not be with yo' ass."

"I never thought I'd see the day you left me for a bitch, you played house with for a season. How could you do this to me? Don't you know how much I love you?" Willow broke down.

Bilaal felt like shit for breaking up with Willow for good, but it was time. He was tired of going through the motions. Seeing Beautii only brought those feelings to surface quicker than he anticipated, but little did Willow know, this day was coming sooner than she thought. Ever since the day Beautii left him, he'd felt like a part of him would never be the same. Seeing her made him feel alive again.

"I know I hurt you, and I apologize for letting this shit between us get so far. I should have been honest with you about where I stood, and I wasn't. You ain't deserve none of that shit, but I gotta do what's best for me. I can't live my life like this no more."

"Muthafucka! Yo' ass is barely here, and when you are, all you wanna do is fuck then go back in them streets. This shit gone explode in your face, then you gon' wanna run back to me when it does. Just know if you leave, ain't no coming back. I'ma be just as done with your ass as you are with me."

"I can live with my decision," Bilaal said with no regrets, then turned towards Willow, and wrapped his arms around her as she broke down. "I gotta go," he kissed Willow's forehead and said.

Willow sniffled, and wiped her tears away. Looking him square in the eyes, she prophesied. "You mark this day, the day you left your family to chase a fantasy. She doesn't love you anymore, but you're too damn selfish to see that. All this shit is gonna blow up in your face. When it does, I want you to remember I told you so. Don't bring your ass back to this house again unless it's for one of our kids. Karma's gonna have a field day on your ass."

Bilaal felt every word Willow spat so deeply he caught a chill and became speechless. He watched as Willow exited his car, and walked towards her door with her head down. He knew he'd dismantled her heart in the worst way, but he couldn't live a lie any longer. Especially not after seeing his one and only love, Beautii. Bilaal grabbed his phone out of his pocket, then called his homeboy Justin.

"Yo'," Justin answered on the third ring. "What's good my nigga?"

"Ain't shit my dude. I'm 'bout to send you a name, and I need you to forward me everything that comes up in the Groove City area. I'm talking phone numbers, addresses, place of employment, and anything else that comes up."

"When you need this information back?"

"As soon as you can get it."

"Say less. You got a picture?"

"Yea, I'll send that too."

"Bet."

Bilaal ended the call and shot Justin a text immediately after.

Bilaal:
Beautii Hamilton

> Justin:
> I got cha.

---

***Two Weeks Later...***

Vertiginous confusion consumed Bilaal's sober thoughts as he sat in his smoke gray, 1971 Ford Mustang GT500, contemplating his next move. Two years was a long time to be away from the one person in the world who held your heart. Bilaal had a lot of time to think, and identify precisely where he went wrong in his and Beautii's previous relationship. *If only I can get her to hear me out.* Forceful. Selfish. Bold. Bilaal had been extremely aggressive in his approach with Beautii, and it hadn't gotten him anywhere.

After seeing Beautii at Langston & Suks he'd found it impossible to function without at least having a conversation with her. He'd thought of a million different ways he wanted to apologize to her, bought her some expensive gifts, and had even written her a few letters. Unsure of which strategy would work best in his pursuit, he hoped like hell that one thing or the other would work in his favor. The look in Beautii's eyes at the restaurant was enough to make the average man walk away and never return. However, that just wasn't in Bilaal's character to back down easily. He was wrong two years ago when he'd mishandled Beautii's trust, and he was dead wrong again for stepping to her despite being on a date with Willow. The truth of the matter was that it was senseless to try teaching an old dog new tricks.

It was six o'clock in the evening, and finally Beautii had

reached the end of her work day. Bilaal had called around to every law office in Groove City, California pretending to be looking for representation, but was lowkey trying to track Beautii down. After his eighth attempt, he located Beautii's place of employment, then hopped on the highway as he anticipated seeing the love of his life one more time. Bilaal had been waiting for her to get off work for the last five hours. Watching as she hopped into her vehicle, Bilaal slowly pulled out into traffic, and trailed her for almost forty-five minutes.

Bilaal waited for about an hour before pulling up, and parking his car behind Beautii's. Taking a deep breath, Bilaal prepared for his presence to be rejected. He knew it would take time to tear down the walls Beautii had built to protect herself against him. At the very least he just wanted her to hear him out, and he needed to see her pretty face again; he had missed her immensely. Exiting his car, he swaggered towards Beautii's front door in a relaxed manner. As if he didn't have a care in the world, he scanned his surroundings, then knocked on her door.

Seconds later, Beautii washed her hands, dried them with a paper towel, then made her way to the door. "Just a second," she called out, before opening it. "Who is it?"

Bilaal thought that if he answered her question, she wouldn't open the door. So, he stood there silently. Hoping she'd just open the door.

Standing on her tippy toes, Beautii looked through the peephole, and recognized Bilaal standing there with a smirk she wanted to smack clean from his fine ass face. Swinging the door open, she asked. "What are you doing here? How did you find me?"

"Why the hell you tryna hide from a nigga?" Bilaal quizzed, gazing deep into Beautii's eyes.

"Don't play with me, Bilaal. How did you find me?" Beautii folded her arms, and asked.

"I got connections, damn. What's with all the questions? This really how you tryna carry a man you said you love?"

"Loved." Beautii corrected. "I've moved on and so should you." Beautii suggested, meaning every word. "Surely, if you were as connected as you say you are; I know you have my number too. So, why didn't you just call me?"

"I could have called, but I wanted to see you. I miss you, baby. I mean damn! You act like you ain't been missing me too."

"Look, this isn't the best time, I'm in the middle of cooking." Beautii digressed, stepping back from the door. "I had a long day today, Bilaal. I just wanna finish cooking this food, take a bath, and lay down."

"Listen, baby. I'm here now. You've already stood here talking to me longer than you wanted to. Can I come in?" Bilaal pleaded. "I bought you a few things I know you like. Just let me talk to you for a minute. I promise I'll leave when you ask me to. I just want you to hear me out."

Beautii wared within herself as she contemplated her decision. "I don't have time to do this song and dance with you anymore. I'm not the same woman anymore. I don't-"

"You're right," Bilaal countered. "I don't deserve anymore of your time, but I'm hoping you'll lend me some of it anyway. I don't deserve shit from you after the way I've treated you in the past, but I've changed too."

"Come in Bilaal, but you can't stay long." Beautii agreed, stepping back, allowing him to enter her home. "Take your shoes off at the door." Beautii instructed, then walked toward the kitchen.

Bilaal obliged, then followed her trail into the kitchen.

"This is a nice place you got here," Bilaal looked around and complimented.

"Thank you," Beautii said, reaching for the already stuffed salmon, and placing it into the oven. "So, what is it you're so eager to talk to me about?" She asked, while searching through one of the kitchen drawers to find her potato peeler.

Bilaal sat in the chair across from Beautii, and admired the way her skin glowed, and her eyes naturally sparkled.

"Why are you staring at me?"

"I can't look at you no more?"

Beautii side eyed him, hoping this wasn't him trying to run game on her. She'd heard it all before. "Are you serious right now?"

"Shit, you been runnin' from a nigga for two years."

"Evolving. I've been focused on myself and evolving in all aspects of my life."

"I can dig it, but did you have to abandon a nigga to do all'lat?"

"I chose me for one, Bilaal." Beautii told him truthfully. "If I had to do it all over again, I'd still make the same decision."

Bilaal nodded his head and bit his tongue because he felt himself getting pissed off by Beautii's honesty. She wasn't holding back any punches, and the truth she spat felt like daggers to his heart.

"If you give me a chance, I can be better for you."

"You had several, and you blew them all," Beauty rinsed off the three potatoes she peeled, then started cutting them up so she could bake them.

"I know I've made a lot of mistakes, and to be honest, ain't shit I can say to justify all the fucked up shit I did. All I can do is show you through my actions that I'm not the same man you left two years ago."

Beautii laughed. "Nigga wasn't you just with the same

woman you were cheating on me with two years ago when I saw you at Langston & Suks?" Beautii asked. "Is that your baby she's carrying?"

Bilaal wanted to lie so bad, but he knew if he did, that would only make things worse for him. "Yes."

"How many kids do you have now?" Beautii curiously asked, while sliding her baking sheet in the oven.

"I have a son, and a daughter on the way," Bilaal revealed, while Beautii stood at the sink and washed her hands. Creeping up behind her, Bilaal wrapped his arms around her waist, and nestled his head in the crease of her neck. Inhaling deeply, Bilaal filled his nasal passage with her scent.

Momentarily, Beautii closed her eyes, and allowed herself to enjoy Bilaal's embrace. She hadn't been touched in two years, and was undoubtedly enjoying her journey of celibacy. However, the mix of Bilaal's *Creed* cologne, and the feel of his erection, caused her hormones to run rampant. "You need to leave now."

Kissing the side of Beautii's neck. "Tell me you ain't miss a nigga, and the way I used to eat that pretty pussy, and fuck you all night long. Tell me you don't want me to fuck the shit out of you again. Have you gripping the sheets, screamin' a nigga name." Bilaal spoke with his lips pressed against her neck, softly kissing her again. Beautii was so angry at her body, and the way it betrayed her.

Like it was yesterday, Beautii remembered the way Bilaal used to fuck her silly, and his tongue game was out of this world. The feeling of his hands cuffing her breast with one hand, then moving south with the other until tucked inside of her panties. Without reserve, Bilaal's middle finger swiped across her clit. "Ahh. Sssss," Beautii moaned, involuntarily.

"Mmhmm. You want me to fuck you again? Go ahead and release that nut, baby. I know you need that shit."

"Stop!" Beautii came back to her senses, and protested. Although her body had betrayed her, her mind reminded her of the reason she left him to begin with. The one thing he consistently did well was fuck her. If only he could've treated her right. Beautii simply required more, and she refused to settle for less. All movement stopped in that instant, and Bilaal slowly moved his hand out of the front of Beautii's pants. "I can't do this. I need you to leave now.

Bilaal backed up and allowed Beautii the space she needed to turn around and face him. With hooded eyes, he raised his hand to his mouth, and licked Beautii's essence from his fingers. "You sure that's what you want me to do? I got what you need, baby. Let me give it to you." Bilaal pleaded.

Beautii whipped her hands across her face, walked past Bilaal, and took her stuffed salmon out of the oven. Catching a glimpse of the sun setting through her peripheral vision, she was reminded that at the conclusion of everyday; she had the power to choose how it ended. "Don't pop up over here unannounced again. I don't feel like giving us a second chance is the best decision for me. I'm trying to move forward in my life, and I can't do that looking backwards. Our time passed Bilaal, and I'm not inclined to reopen any chapters in my life I had to beg God to deliver me from. I'm sorry, but I just can't do this with you again."

The hurt in Bilaal's eyes was impossible to miss. Beautii remembered the times she used to think about how much joy she'd get the day she got to witness the day his heart got broken the way he broke hers. She knew it was wrong to wish hurt on other people, but that was her truth. Now that she saw it, she'd be lying if she said she enjoyed it. She didn't.

"I'ma accept this shit for now. I'ma give you a little more time to realize I'm the only man you'll ever need," Bilaal walked towards the door. "I'll be back for you soon, Beautii," He nodded. "Next time I'ma make sure my offer is impossible to resist."

    Walking out of the door, Bilaal knew he wasn't about to give up that easily. He also understood if he continued to push, Beautii would continue to pull away. A wise man once said, *"You gotta know when to hold, know when to fold, and when to walk away."* This was especially true with Beautii.

## CHAPTER SIX

### BEAUTII HAMILTON

The faint hum of Beautii's washer and dryer running at the same time echoed in the background, as she lay awake gazing at her ceiling. She fought relentlessly to settle her emotions, and still her aroused hormones. Bilaal had selfishly invaded her space, and as much as she wanted to place all the blame on him; she had to own her part in the fiasco. Truthfully, she'd already had her closure when it came to Bilaal, but she allowed him to come into her space because she was considerate. She knew he wouldn't leave her alone until she heard him out. She didn't anticipate the move Bilaal had made on her, and she was more pissed at herself than him.

She'd set a standard for herself when she met him, but lowered it for a night of pleasure, which resulted in years of manipulation, heartache, and unnecessary drama. She hated that once again, she'd set the bar high, and in a moment's weakness, she'd let her guard down for instant pleasure. *If you don't stand for something, you'll fall for anything*, Beautii reminded herself. She knew this, but had forgotten the minute she felt Bilaal's hardened erection against her ass. All her common sense voluntarily left the second she felt his hands moving south, his minty breath against her neck, and his wet tongue swirling in circles on her neck.

    Charming, thuggish, and fine as hell were just a few things that once turned Beautii on about him once upon a time. Beautii had taken time out to mature and elevate her mind. She'd dared to dream bigger, desire more, and maintained her chastity while doing it. The act was commendable, noble even, but, in the face of adversity- she reverted to what was familiar. Bilaal had blown his chances with Beautii. The weakness he'd uncovered within her, left her feeling cheap and vacant.

> *"You can't beg God to heal you, then stay loyal to what's hurting you."*

    Beautii remembered what her mother told her when things didn't work out with her first love in high school. His name was Alonzo Ross. She'd forgiven him for hurting her, but she'd never forget the year of depression she went through. It was a secret that she and her mother kept between them because Bruce would've paid Alonzo a visit for hurting his daughter. Bruce was with all the smoke when it came to his wife and his daughter. Since then, Beautii had made a vow to herself that she'd refuse to inherit dysfunction in her future. She'd vowed to learn and adapt to new ways of living that didn't involve her repeating the things she lived through.

    At twenty-five years young, Beautii had been through some things, but she'd been determined to conquer all aspects of her life. Her father had been her reason to fight through every obstacle and come out victorious. His freedom, his presence in her life, and the fact that she needed him was enough to make her resilient. The fight for her father's freedom hadn't been an easy one, but thanks to God; he'd made it out unscathed. The buzzing from the dryer and her washer sounded at the same time. Raising up from her fluffy pillow, she sat on the side of the bed, and slid both feet inside of her house slippers.

"Whew!" Beautii blurted out after standing to her feet and yawning. Making her way to the hallway, she switched her clothes over, then picked up the laundry basket so she could fold the clothes up in her room. Sitting the basket on her bed, she walked over to the window and opened her blinds.

Beautii greeted the morning sun with a smile, then walked back over to her bed. Grabbing her remote, she scrolled to the spotify app on her TV and pressed play on the latest playlist she created just weeks prior.

*"How do I get to the heal? Hard to assess how I feel nowadays. Think in my mind, something changed. Struggling here, in the interface. In between self-love and the loss of you. Moment in time and I know the truth…"*

Alex Isley & Jack Dine's *Still Wonder* spilled lowly from the TV speakers, instantly complementing the peaceful mood Beautii was already in. Just as she sat down and started folding her clothes her phone rang. Reaching over to the nightstand, she answered on the second ring.

"Hey daddy!" Beautii squealed excitedly.

"What's goin' on, beautiful?" Bruce answered. "What you doin' on this good Sunday?"

"Nothing much. I just took some clothes out of the dryer. I'll be chillaxin' for the rest of the day."

"Chillaxin'?"

"Yes, daddy. It's short for chillin' and relaxin'," Beautii giggled.

Bruce shook his head and chuckled. "Next time pick one or the other."

"Oh lawd! Daddy you gotta keep up."

"Your mother and I want you to come by today. I'ma put some chicken, steak, and ribs on the grill."

"And, what mama gone make?"

"Her famous mac-n-cheese, cabbage, and potato salad," Bruce revealed. "If you hurry up and get here, you can make me some banana pudding."

"Today's your lucky day. I made some last night. I'll just bring that."

"Umm, so you was gon' keep it all to yourself, huh? You know that ain't right."

"Not at all. You just spoiled your own surprise."

Bruce chuckled. "You love your old man, huh?"

"Of course, I do."

"Hurry up and get here, so I can tear you up on this here pool table."

"You been drinking this early, daddy?"

"Just had one of those mimosas ya mama be makin' in the morning. Why?"

"Because you can't be in your right mind, thinking I'm 'bout to let you tear me up." Beautii cracked up laughing. "You may need a few practice rounds. You may be a little rusty."

"You betta stop yo stuff girl. Something's in life just come natural."

"Alright, we'll see about that."

"Alright, I'll see you when you get here. Love you."

"Love you too, daddy."

Beautii concluded their call, finished folding clothes, then remade her bed. Flicking the light on, she entered her walk-in closet. Within the last two years, Beautii's wardrobe had grown stupendously. Her style had enhanced now that she'd reached a high level of financial freedom. She loved labels like Chanel, FENDI, Balenciaga, and Louis Vuiton. However, she loved to support black owned labels too. Scanning her closet, Beautii locked her eyes on a brand new pair of high waist denim jeans, brown top, and nude colored sandals. Reaching up on her tippy toes, Beautii grabbed her cream white quilted caviar Chanel purse. Then hopped in the shower to prepare for a day of fun with her parents.

*Two Hours Later...*

Beautii hit the locks on her black on black, Mercedes Maybach Exelero. This was her brand new baby, and she called it Giselle. Ever since she was a little girl, she watched her parents name all their cars; it was a tradition in their family. Placing the cooler that secured the pan of banana pudding she made in the trunk, Beautii got in the car, set the temperature, then scrolled to her favorite playlist she created on Apple Music. Ding! Beautii looked down at her text notification that came through.

*Blyss Valentino:*
*Good morning. I know it's Sunday, but can you meet me at the office later on?*
*Beautii:*
*Good morning! I'm on my way to my parents house now, and I won't be back until around nine o'clock tonight. Do you wanna come to my house instead?*
*Blyss Valentino:*
*See you then. Enjoy your day.*

An unapologetic smile spread across Beautii's face for reasons she still hadn't sifted through yet. Blyss was a very powerful man, who was dangerously attractive. Everything about him screamed regality. His presence was felt when he walked into a room, his scent was hypnotizing, and prestige dripped heavily through his pores. Men like Blyss carried silent authority that couldn't be infiltrated; impossible to dilute. His ambiguity spoke volumes. His intricacy was so precise, so strategic, it spilled over into the way he dressed, his poise, and the way he conducted business. Blyss' reticence since meeting Beautii had slowly dwindled, and she enjoyed getting to know the fiber of his character layer by layer.

Beautii often questioned in law school if she'd ever grow weary in her profession, but everyday she worked beside Blyss, the journey had been well worth it. Afterall, doing what you love isn't really considered work, if you love what you're doing. The proverb suggested *'You can't have your cake, and eat it too.'* Beautii; however, somehow managed to obtain extreme favor. Beautii nodded her head as Musiq Soulchild's *So Beautiful* streamed through the car speakers. She switched gears and began her road trip to her parents house.

---

"Knock, knock," Beautii announced, after letting herself in her parents home. Instantly, she scanned and took in the small changes her mother had made to the house since her father had been home from prison. Entranced at the door, Beautii closed her eyes and took in the savory smell of home cooked food, and barbeque from the grill. It was just like old times. Beautii didn't realize how much she missed being at home, in her comfort zone with her parents.

"Beautii queen, is that you?" Mea, Beautii's mother called, as she rounded the corner.

Opening her eyes, Beautii answered her mom with a smile. "Hey ma! You look so pretty," Beautii complimented. "I love this new living room set, and these plants are beautiful."

Mea didn't believe in buying fake plants to put in her house. Not everybody had the patience to take care of real plants. It was a gift that in most cases was handed down, and traditional. This was the case when it came to Mea. She had a few vine plants, but her favorites were the plants that survived in low lighting, and of course her aloe vera plants.

"Thank you! Now come give your mama some love," Mea smiled and welcomed Beautii into her warm embrace. "You look gorgeous too, Beautii. What is it that you have on? It smells so good."

"Thanks mom. It's called J'adore."

"Umm, this would be a good gift for my birthday or mother's day," Mea hinted.

"I think it's a good gift to give just because," Beautii said, handing her mother a peach colored gift bag.

"Oh my goodness, thank you so much," Mea exclaimed. "How'd you know I'd want this perfume?"

"'Cause I know you. I'm always thinking of you, and trying to find ways to bless you. I know I probably don't say it enough, but I love you so much." Beautii kissed her mother's cheek. "Now let me get this banana pudding in the refrigerator."

"I'm sorry, I don't know how I missed that cooler in your hand. Come on." Mea led the way into the kitchen.

*"Driftin' on a memory. Ain't no place I'd rather be, then with you…"*

Beautii observed her father through the window jamming to the Isley brothers song *For the Love of You*. A smile quickly crept upon Beautii's face. Her heart was instantly warmed, as she and her mother stood back gazing through the window. Bruce was standing in front of the grill, flipping meat, and holding his cognac in the opposite hand. He was truly in his element, and both Mea and Beautii loved to see it.

"I'm so proud of you, Beautii. Thank you for bringing your father back home to me. I couldn't survive much longer without him out here with me," Mea spoke honestly. She appreciated her daughter, and knew if it wasn't for her, Bruce would still be behind prison bars.

"Thank you, ma. It wasn't a stretch at all. We all need each other, I'm just grateful God intervened, and for Blyss' help. Without their help I don't know how I could have possibly pulled any of it off." Beautii told her mother honestly.

"You're so humble," Mea wrapped her arm around Beautii's waist, and pulled her closer. "That's one of the many things I admire about you. Don't short change yourself though. You are an exceptional lawyer. Remarkable. If it weren't so, you wouldn't be working with the best attorney in Groove City." Mea nudged Beautii with her hip, then grabbed the cooler from Beautii. "I'll put the banana pudding in the refrigerator. Go out there and speak to your father, I'm almost done here."

"Are you sure you don't need any help in here before I go?"

"Nope… I'm good in here. I'll be out there in a bit," Mea dismissed, sitting the banana pudding in the refrigerator.

*"Lovely as a ray of sun, that touches me when the mornin' comes. Feels good to me, yeah. My love and me. Smoother than a gentle breeze. Flowin' through my mind with ease. Soft as can be…"*

Easing up behind her father, Beautii harmonized with her father. Turning around, his eyes filled with love and admiration.

"My Beautii," Bruce welcomed with a light chuckle and opened arms. "It's about time you came to see your old man. You lookin' good." He complimented, then closed down the top of the grill. "We got some *Stella Rosa* and wine coolers in the ice box over there. Help yourself," he offered.

"Thanks daddy, let me go get some now." Beautii went inside the house and grabbed herself a glass and a few ice cubes, then came back out and poured herself some wine. Sitting down on the double papasan patio chair, Beautii sat back and crossed her ankles. Taking a long sip of her wine, her eyes instantly overlooked the inground pool. Ever since Beautii had moved into Blyss' house, she'd developed this immense attraction to water views. They provided her with an undeniable mental escape, and an oasis of tranquility.

Beautii was unlike some who received promotions in the world, but didn't have the mental capacity, or character to maintain their position. She prayed earnestly for elevation and growth in her mentality, and with much meditation and dedication to becoming her best self; her results have been notable. Bruce took the ribs off of the grill, and took them in the house for Mea to put barbecue sauce on them. He returned with a few pieces of steak and chicken. Once placing the meat on the rack, he washed his hands in some soapy water he had sitting on the table beside him, then walked over to sit with Beautii.

"What's going on, Beautii. How's everything going at the firm?"

"Everything is good daddy. I love everything about the office and all the people I work around. It's been a breeze, and much like my partner, I've been on a winning streak." Beautii gushed and sang.

"Now that's what I like to hear. Congratulations," Bruce raised his glass in the air for a toast. "What's going on with Blyss? I thought you would have invited him over by now."

"Why would I do that?" Beautii bit down on her bottom lip and asked.

"You still in denial, Beautii?" Bruce took a swig of his cognac, then sat up to refill his glass with more brown liquor.

"Denial?"

"You know you like that man. I sensed it when we went out to eat, and I noticed the way you were looking at him. I know that look."

Beautii laughed, then took a sip of her wine. "That meat smells like it may be getting a little scorched, you better go check on that."

"Scorched?" Bruce looked at Beautii like she had lost her mind. "Since when have you ever known me to burn anything? You got me confused wit'cha mama.

"Check with me about what?" Mea asked, sneaking up behind them sipping on a cocktail of her own.

"Daddy said you be burning up the food," Beautii said, then started laughing.

"What!" Bruce looked up from the grill. "Baby, now you know I love your cooking. Who you gon' believe?" Bruce asked, while doing his best not to laugh.

Bruce and Beautii started rolling.

"Y'all come on in the house so we can eat before it gets too late," Mea said, then turned to walk back in the house.

"Trouble maker," Beautii whispered as she walked past her father. He laughed again, as he flipped the chicken over. Contrary to the little joke Bruce and Beautii had going on,

Mea was a great cook. There wasn't one thing Bruce could think of that she couldn't make well.

Thirty minutes later, Bruce joined the dining room table with Mea and Beautii, then blessed the food.

"Don't eat too much 'cause I don't want no excuses when it comes to this beat down you 'bout to receive on the pool table," Bruce boasted, then took a bite of his ribs.

"Did you take your vitamins today? You know you gettin' old now, and you can't be standing up for long periods of time." Beautii shot back, giving her father a side eye.

"Yea, a'ight." Bruce nodded his head, and continued to eat.

"I tell you what. If you beat me, I'll buy you a new Rolex," Beautii raised the stakes.

"And, if you beat me, I'll take you to Disney World." Bruce promised.

"Oh, you got yourself a deal." Beautii agreed with a huge smile. Ever since Beautii was a little girl, Bruce took her to Disney World every year. They always had such a good time, and Beautii always looked forward to spending that time with her father. It never got old because it was never about the rides, and all the kiddy things that took place there. Quality time. Love. Bonding. It was about being present for each other. Bruce took Beautii on trips across the world to instill standards, boost expectations, and show her how a man was supposed to treat her. Mea couldn't ask for a better husband or father for her daughter. Bruce was a rare black man, and both Beautii and Mea cherished him. Once done with their food, Beautii helped her mom clean the kitchen, then met Bruce in the family room. Tony! Toni! Toné! *It Never Rains* thumped through the floor standing speakers as Mea and Beautii walked in.

"Oh, now this is my song," Mea announced, then walked

up to Bruce and started dancing. Beautii grabbed her pool stick, then did her little two-step while her parents had their moment. These were small things to most people, but for Beautii these small memories meant the world to her.

Beautii danced over to the mini bar, and made herself a cranberry and vodka infused cocktail. While taking a sip from her glass, she admired her parents' unique connection. *I'll be glad when real love finally finds me.* Beautii had already experienced the lows of love, and although she was healed, the residue still remained. Memories of being loved wrong replayed in the recesses of her mind, especially in her dreams.

"You ready to buy my new Rolex?" Bruce asked, while putting chalk on the tip of his pool stick.

Beautii laughed. "Yeah a'ight. Rack 'em up old man. You can go first too."

"You sure about that? You know I'm not gon' show you no mercy," Bruce told Beautii, then got in position to break the balls. Making his first shot, the stripped 7 and 4 ball went into the far left pocket.

"Lucky shot. Looks like somebody's been practicing," Beautii stood back and observed his skill.

"I told you, I'm a natural. I don't need luck," Bruce winked his eye at Beautii. "Red striped 5 ball, far right, side pocket," Bruce called his shot, and missed it by a hair. "Hold on one second, I gotta watch you," Bruce said, before answering his phone. "What's good, man? You made it?"

"Yea, I've been at the door for about ten minutes."

"We got this music turned up, but hold up a second. The wife is coming now to let you in."

Beautii took her shot, making two solid balls go in the right side pocket, and one in the far left pocket. "Yea, now what was that, you were saying?" Beautii emphasized, with her hand positioned behind her ear.

"Gon' and take ya' shot. The game ain't over yet," Bruce dismissed, inwardly salty about Beautii's shot.

"Oh, so you tryna rush me now. I understand," Beautii laughed at her father.

"Good evening, Sir!" Blyss announced, energetically as he entered the family room.

At the speed of light, Beautii's head turned at the sound of Blyss' voice. *What the hell?* Beautii was perplexed with the reality of Blyss Valentino standing in her parents house, embracing her father.

"What's good, Beautii," Blyss greeted with a sly grin, walking in her direction, then wrapping her in a friendly embrace.

"It's always good to see you, but what's this about? I told you I'd call you when I got back home to discuss the case." Beautii said nicely.

"He's here because we invited him over," Bruce revealed. "Anyone who played a part in getting me released from that hell hole I was locked in is family. He said seriously. "Besides, I needed some competition," Bruce gestured towards Blyss.

Beautii wasn't cognizant of the twenty thousand dollars Blyss had slipped to her father before leaving Langston & Suks. It was a huge solid to do for a stranger, but due to Beautii being such an asset to Blyss' law firm; he viewed it as a light investment. Beautii had been on a winning streak just like Blyss, and it had everything to do with her own skill. She was a beast in the courtroom. Bruce and Blyss had been talking a lot, mainly because he needed to fill out the man his daughter was around everyday a little bit more now that he was free.

"Are you hungry?" Mea asked. "I can go fix your plate whenever you're ready."

"Yes ma'am. I'd appreciate that," Blyss replied.

Meanwhile, Beautii slipped into a daze, and despite how intelligent, intuitive, and dazzling she was; Blyss made her nervous. As her father took his turn, Beautii sized up Blyss' tall, slim, athletic build. Garbed in dark denim jeans, a purple and grey checkered button down shirt, and a pair of J's; Blyss stood to the side and watched Bruce take his second shot. Beautii was so captivated by his debonair, she didn't even realize that it was her turn.

"Beautii, it's your turn." Bruce said, stepping back from the table, observing his daughter and Blyss. Bruce was a wise man, and he knew his daughter through and through. Beautii may have been able to hide from many people, mask her attraction to Blyss, and act as if everything was peachy; but he knew she'd been through something. That blow up at Langston and Suks was a lot deeper than she put on. When she was ready, Bruce knew she'd come to him. He didn't insert himself in Beautii's life like a lot of overbearing fathers did. He'd sized Bilaal up from a distance, and understood Beautii's attraction to him; he also knew he wasn't the one for his daughter.

Observing the table, Beautii planted her feet, then bent down, getting eye level with the ball she wanted to land in the right side pocket. Controlling the pool stick with her left hand, she eased the stick back and forth between her pointer and middle finger; with force she hit the cue ball and hit the solid 2 in the side pocket. Blyss was impressed, especially since he'd never witnessed a woman play pool with such skill. Beautii continued to hit ball after ball every pocket in sight, until only the solid 8 ball was left.

"When we going to Disney world, daddy," Beautii laughed, rubbing in the fact that she'd put in work on the table. Bruce remained silent, as Mea and Blyss cracked up on the sidelines. Hitting the 8 ball in the opposite left pocket,

Beautii won the game. "You want a rematch?" Beautii smiled.

Bruce took a long swig from his glass before replying. "Good game." He nodded. "I taught you well. Set it up and we can go whenever you want."

Beautii walked back over to the mini bar, reached inside of her purse, and grabbed a black box out of it. "Here you go, daddy. I got this for you," Beautii handed her father the box and said.

"What's this, Beautii?"

"Open it up and see."

Bruce's eyes bulged in surprise when he saw the Daytonas Rolex. "Damn right!" Bruce stopped in his tracks and said, while taking it out of the box and putting it on to see how it looked on his arm. "This is a classic right here. Look," Bruce gestured towards Blyss.

Getting up from the couch, Blyss walked over to view the watch. Raising his arm up, Blyss looked down at his wrist, comparing his watch to Bruce's. "That's a nice one there, real talk."

"Thank you again, Beautii. Me and your mother will be right back." Bruce informed his daughter, before leaving.

"Of course, daddy. You and mom deserve all the best things life has to offer."

"Thank you, Beautii, We love you so much," Mea, Beautii's mom replied, then kissed her cheek.

"You play pool?" Beautii asked Blyss, while racking up all the balls from the side pockets.

"I can do a little something on a green top table," Blyss replied.

"Let's see what you got then," Beautii said, before hitting the ball.

"Mhm," Blyss replied confidently. He wasn't a big shit

talker, but rest assured he'd studied Beautii style and form from the sideline. He'd studied everything about Beautii for the last two years. In order to mesh well in a partnership, it's imperative to know your partners strengths and weaknesses. This wisdom is what kept Blyss on his toes as he positioned everyone on his team to win across the board. Beautii wasn't an amateur, and Blyss was competitive as hell.

Beautii took her shot the second time, and missed purposely. She needed to see what type of pool player Blyss was. Chalking the tip of his pool stick, Blyss walked over to the far left, then took his shot. Hitting the four balls in at one time, Blyss walked over to the opposite end of the table. Impressed. Beautii was moved to silence as she stood back and observed his technique. She'd broken one of the top five rules in pool; never underestimate your opponent. Blyss hit all his balls in the side slots with little to no effort at all. The one shot Beautii made at the beginning was the only one she made for the rest of the game.

"Rematch! You tricked me." Beautii exclaimed in utter disbelief.

Blyss chuckled. "You thought I couldn't play, huh?"

"Tuh," Beautii was pissed at herself for not putting her best foot forward. This was one sport she didn't like to lose. Unlike most sports where only physical energy was exerted, pool involved a hint of chess due to the amount of mental strength necessary to strategize and win against your opponent. Beautti removed the rack, Blyss broke the balls, and landed two balls in at the same time. After his fourth shot, he finally missed the ball he aimed for. Taking her first shot, Beautii took a risk at a rare shot, and hit the 8 ball in on her first shot; ending the game with a win. "Ahhh. Yes Lawd!" Beautii excitedly yelled.

"Lucky shot. Let's get this tie breaker crackin' tho," Blyss dusted his shoulders off, and said. He loved to be challenged, and Beautii presented exactly that. Nothing was worse than a woman who had nothing going for herself besides good looks.

Beautii burst out laughing at Blyss' disposition, the tables had turned quickly. "So, what was it that you needed to discuss with me?" Beautii simultaneously changed the subject and made Blyss a drink.

"It's about Trevin Louis' case. I gave it to you about two weeks ago. Did you ever get a chance to look it over?"

"Actually, I did." Beautii passed Blyss his cognac infused cocktail, then took a sip of her own.

"Yea? Tell me what you thought," Blyss inquired, while taking a swallow from his glass.

"Treven Louis was his name right?" Beautii quizzed, as she broke the balls again.

"That's his name."

"I think he got himself in a tight situation that's next to impossible to wiggle out of." Beautii said honestly. "His bodily fluids were left on the crime scene. I can't see him getting anything less than twenty five years to life in prison. That was an extremely heinous crime. I don't think it's in our best interest to take his case on."

"Yea, I thought the same thing until a man named Westley Cannon called me," Blyss revealed. "He said he wanted to take the stand, and admit to both murders."

"How will we get around the saliva that was close to the crime scene?"

"Louis was there earlier that same day. His story and the new found evidence aligned perfectly."

Beautii's knowing look revealed her train of thoughts without her having to say one word. Blyss shrugged his shoulders. "Hey, that's his life. If this is how he wants to live out the rest of his days that's on him."

Beautii thought it over. "Well, let's get to the back partner," Beautii raised her glass in the air and clinked glasses with Blyss. So much was on the line with this case, and 2.5 million was a hefty amount to add to their bank accounts after splitting the money. That was one thing about Blyss Valentino, he was gone get to the money, but he was gone break bread with his team every time. He made sure everybody at his table ate too. They played for another two hours before deciding they were ready to hit the road.

※※※

"So you really took a flight to spend a few hours with me and my family?" Beautii asked, leaning her seat back a little.

"Yea, I was running late, and figured there was no need for us to ride in two separate vehicles." Blyss shrugged. They were two hours into the three hour drive back to Groove City, so Blyss finally addressed the situation that occurred at Langston & Sucks. "Can I ask you a personal question?" Blyss tested his boundaries.

"Sure. What's up?" Beautii replied, glancing at Blyss, then focused back on the road.

"Who was that nigga that approached you at Langston & Suks?"

Inwardly, Beautii cringed at the memory of Bilaal. She'd just freed her mind from his memory, and now here it was again.

"It's cool if you don't wanna talk about it," Blyss offered her a way out. It wasn't his intention to make her feel uncomfortable.

"No, it's fine." Beautii inhaled deeply then exhaled a steady breath. "That was my ex, Bilaal. We were together for two years and things between us didn't work out. He was a serial cheater, a narcissist, and the ultimate womanizer." Beautii explained.

"Damn. I could tell that nigga wasn't 'bout shit."

"How?"

"When I looked at that nigga, his eyes wavered. Anytime a nigga can't hold eye contact, especially a territorial muthafucka, he's a fuckin' coward. Real rap. Ain't nothing worse than a nigga who wanna control shit, but ain't got shit to stand on. No real power, no real respect, just a flock of women with low self-esteem. The shit is sickening."

At that moment, Beautii thanked the Creator for growth. Two years ago, Beautii would have cussed Blyss out for the statement he'd just made. The woman she'd grown to be practiced taking accountability, walked in truth, and had learned how to cultivate herself in self-love. She also understood the type of man Blyss was. He didn't sugar coat anything, he was straight forward in his approach, and he was a powerful alpha. "You're right. I should have left him the first time he cheated on me, but I didn't because I thought I could teach him. I thought that if I loved him right, he'd change for me. Unfortunately, things just didn't pan out that way." Beautii took accountability for her bad judgment. "My main focus overall was to get through law school, I couldn't afford to get distracted, so I kept him around for reasons. I needed to make my next move, my best. Now it's been two years, and I haven't looked back since."

Strength. Confidence. Fire. Peace. Blyss felt her strength, he heard her confidence. Behind her eyes, he witnessed fire enforced by passion, and the peace Beautii had found consumed Blyss. No woman had ever made him feel vulnerable before, but Beautii made Blyss yearn for a deeper connection with her. Blyss had two contracted open relationships with no strings attached, and the thought to settle had always been nonexistent. He'd guarded his heart, and swore any woman who could plow through all the defenses he put up; he'd marry her. "One of the best decisions you'll ever make in life is to never look back. The past is the past for a reason."

"You're right," Beautii agreed. "I know it's late, but can I ask a favor before you go?" Beautii asked once she pulled in front of her house.

"Yea. What's goin' on?" Blyss asked before getting out of Beautii's car.

"The faucet is leaking in the kitchen sink. Can you take a look at it?" Beautii inquired, as she reached in the backseat for her purse.

"Yea, I can do that. I think I left some tools under that sink." Blyss agreed.

## CHAPTER SEVEN

### BLYSS VALENTINO

Blyss was a jack of all trades. While he fixed the issue with the faucet, Beutii went up stairs, and changed into a light brown pair of tights with a matching sports bra. Jhene Aiko's *Moments* vibed through the surround sound speakers, and caused Blyss to look up. As soon as Beautii made it back down stairs, Blyss was drying his hands off.

"Everything is fixed now. Let me know if you have any other issues. If I can't fix it myself, I'll call someone out here to see about it."

"Thank you so much. I've been meaning to tell you, but I've been having my mind on so many other things."

"That's understandable. We lead busy lives."

"We do," Beautii agreed. "Thanks for coming to chill with me and my parents by the way."

"Your pops is good people. We talk all the time since he's been home."

"What?" Beautii couldn't believe what she was hearing. "So, when was yall gone tell me about this?"

Blyss laughed. "I thought you knew." Blyss said, lustfully sizing Beautii up. The way Beautii's skin glowed, and her body filled out the little clothes she wore; Blyss' body begged him to surrender and go with the flow. Beautii's eyes were so alluring, Blyss wondered why he'd never noticed before.

*"So when I call you better answer me. Right now, I need you here on me. No substitute, you the one and only. Please take away the stress I don't need. You got me on my knees, baby, James Brown, please..."*

As if caught in a time warp, Beautii and Blyss' gravitated towards each other. Slowly. Intentionally. Blyss looked at Beautii with so much passion in his eyes, her pupils dilated and her nipples hardened. The feeling of Beautii's skin beneath Blyss' fingertips was like swiping his hands over a sheet of silk, and he needed her to be closer. Resistance was nonexistent. The opening of Beautii's arms gave welcome home vibes, as she pulled him closer. Pressing her sweet lips against his, their tongues did a sexy Brazilian Zouk dance.

*"With you, with you, with you, with you, with you, with you. I get caught in the moment..."*

Caught in the moment, Beautii and Blyss shared a kiss so magical, they both became dizzy with desire. Never in life had the duo wanted anything more than they wanted each other. Jhene Aiko and Big Sean created a masterpiece with *Moments*, because surely they'd succeeded at creating the moment of a lifetime for Beautii and Blyss. They put words to the sentiments of their hearts, and neither wanted it to end. Many times crossing the line had entered both of their minds, but neither ever acted on their urges. Maintaining a good working relationship was imperative, but at the moment their desires overrode their boundaries.

Shattering the moment, Beautii pulled back, and gathered her resolve. "I'm sorry. I shouldn't have done that. I... I... I was..."

"Shhh." Blyss closed the small space Beautii put between them, still caught up. "Ain't shit about this moment, an accident. It may not be the time right now, but when it comes again." Blyss paused, licked his lips, and undressed Beautii with his eyes. "Ain't nothin' in this world gon' stop a nigga from respectfully, disrespecting that pussy." He paused, and bore deep into Beautii's soul. "Nigga done had too many fantasies of pushin' you on my desk and kissing them pretty lips, while sliding my fingers in ya pussy just to see how wet you is. Umhmm, then put it in ya mouth so you can see how good it taste, right before a nigga make u cream in them panties without this dick even in yet." He stepped closer, and caught another whiff of Beautii's intoxicating scent. "I'ma make you grab him, and push it hard inside you 'til you explode all on that muthafucka on the first stroke."

Beautii moaned, unapologetically.

"See that? That pussy been mines. Act like you know." Blyss stepped back a bit, then gazed deep in Beautii's orbs. "I've played my position, now I'm done. Ain't nuthin' stoppin' me no more. Whenever, wherever, however... Come see me. I'ma brand that pussy with love notes, and lullabies from my dick, permanently." Blyss promised, then bent slightly, and stole another kiss. He'd gotten so high off that kiss, the ground felt like it was moving. Without warning, Beautii had unnerved, and discombobulated him at the same time. The feeling of Beautii's body shuddering under his gentle touch, was all the assurance he needed to have.

Two Weeks Later…

    The morning sun peeked through the blinds of Blyss' office with a warm glow. Drinking a cup of Starbucks caramel macchiato, he gathered his thoughts before his first consultation of the day came in. Monday's for many people was the longest day of the week, but for Blyss, Tuesday's were the longest. He preferred to see all his consultations in thirty minute increments on Tuesday morning's starting at seven o'clock sharp until lunch time. The rest of his day was normally consumed with court proceedings, returning phone calls/emails, and several meetings. Working with Beautii had taken a lot of weight off of him, but one thing about Blyss Valentino; he always stayed in his bag.

    Blyss looked down at his rolex, and realized his eight o'clock appointment was running almost fifteen minutes late. One thing Blyss didn't take for granted was his time. He wasn't named amongst the best for nothing. Blyss had his hands in numerous business ventures, so there was hardly ever a dull moment. There was always work to be done, and every minute he spent waiting, he could be doing something else. Walking to his desk, he picked up his phone, and called Jillian.

    "Good morning, Mr. Valentino." Jillian greeted when she answered the phone.

    "Good morning, Jillian. Have you heard anything from James Tiller this morning? His appointment was supposed to start fifteen minutes ago." Blyss greeted, then impatiently inquired.

    "No, he hasn't called, but give me just a second and I'll

call him," Jillian pulled up his information on her computer and assured before disconnecting the call.

Sitting down at his desk, Blyss pulled out his phone, and scrolled to Beautii text thread.

*Blyss:*
*Good morning, Beautiful. Just wanted you to know I'm thinkin' of you.*

*Beautii:*
*Good morning, Blyss. It's good to be thought about. You have a great day.*

*Blyss:*
*It'll be even better if you agree to have a few drinks with me after work this evening.*

*Beautii:*
*I gotta go. Court is about to start. I'll let you know.*

The office phone rang as soon as he put his cell down.

"Blyss Vanlentino," he answered.

"Hey Blyss. I just spoke to James Tiller and got him rescheduled."

"I appreciate that."

"Before you go, someone by the name of Sedora is here to see you." Jillian let him know before he hung up.

"You can send her up." Blyss replied. *Why the hell did she come here without calling me first?* Blyss asked himself. He and Sedora had history, but she'd never done this before.

Moments later, Sedora knocked on the door.

"Come in," Blyss calmly invited.

"Good Morning, handsome," Sedora greeted with a smile. "Long time no see."

"It has," Blyss agreed. "What can I do for you?" Blyss asked.

It's not necessarily what you can do for me. I'm here for what you can do to me." Sedora said seductively. Slowly unbuttoning her shirt, licking her pouty lips. "Come here," she beckoned him with her other hand.

Blyss shook his head and chuckled. "This ain't our agreement, Sedora." He casually reminded her.

"To hell with our agreement. That contract has been ongoing for years, it's about time we make this thing between us official don't you think?"

"Official?"

"Yes, official. Aren't you ready to settle down yet?" Sedora asked. "I thought you'd be the first to break the ice, but you know I don't mind going after what I want," Sedora eased her way closer to Blyss. "And, right now, I want you."

"As tempting as your offer is, I gotta pass Sedora. I'on operate like this." Blyss honestly protested. "The rules I set in place are for a reason. They protect both of us."

"You sure you don't wanna take a walk on the wild side with me? You know I can make it worth your while." Sedora said, dropping down to her knees. She knew giving Blyss head was one of his weaknesses, and her specialty. The sound of heavy breath expelled from his mouth, indicated the weakening of his resolve.

"As of today our contract is terminated, Sedora. I never pegged you as a thirsty woman whose actions become reckless when things don't go her way." Blyss had never been disgusted with Sedora before, but the move she'd made was one Blyss detested. Spontaneity wasn't the problem, but the forceful connotation, and controlling nature of her actions had Blyss seeing Sedora in a different light. It was part of Blyss' nature to be strategic, deliberate, and extremely private. "Leave quietly." Blyss finalized.

"Wow, so you're just going to end things between us because I wanted to surprise you today?" Sedora's voice cracked the moment she felt the coldness of his words. She never anticipated the day Blyss Valentino would sever ties indefinitely with her.

The sound of the office phone ringing incessantly interrupted the onslaught dramatics that Sedora was about to slip into. "Blyss Valentino," he answered, eyes trained on Sedora.

"Your next scheduled consultation just arrived. Would you like for me to send them up?"

"Yes, that'll be fine. Thanks Jillian." Blyss replied before disconnecting the call. "My next consultation is on the way up, so I need you to leave now.

"Fuck you, Blyss. You don't ever have to worry about me again." Bitterness and confusion took root in Sedora's heart, as her vision blurred with the threat of tears as she fixed her blouse, and walked out of Blyss' office.

---

Profound were the thoughts that crossed Blyss' mind after a long days' work, yet still, there was so much to be done. The pleasant notes Sisqó from Dru Hill sang were a welcomed distraction. *Beauty* was the perfect song to match the flow of his thoughts concerning Beautii Hamilton. A few weeks had gone by since the duo shared a kiss so intimate. So intense. So sweet. Blyss was still stuck in a daze, as he envisioned, and replayed the same scene over and over in the recesses of his mind. Off and on throughout the day, he'd heard all the talk about the severe thunderstorm on the forecast. Some even predicted the possibility of the first hurricane Groove City had ever witnessed. Many bought into the theory, some took extreme precautions, while Blyss decided to stay at the office and continue working like he would on any other normal day. Blyss had been living in Groove City for over twenty years, and he hadn't witnessed one rainy day. Blyss was a considerate man, so he'd given Jillian and Beautii the rest of the day off. Sitting at his office desk, Blyss pulled a few files out, then started his research for a case he had coming up for an attempted murder case.

Unbeknownst to Blyss, Beautii stayed at work instead of going home after leaving court. Since moving to Groove City, no matter where Beautii went, God was gracious enough to give her some type of water view. None of them had topped the oasis view she had at her house. Be that as it may, the one she viewed frequently from her work office was wondrous as well. Beautii was fascinated by the warm mixtures of purple, burnt orange, and yellow spread across the sky. She too had heard all the warnings about the coming storm, but like Blyss; she'd ignored them all. The day had been so beautiful, and from where she sat; there was no way a storm was coming anytime soon. Snatching her eyes away from the window, Beautii refocused her attention to her Apple computer. She had a few letters she needed to write and send to her clients while it was on her mind.

Subsequently, Blyss had worked up an appetite about an hour in a half later. Blyss instantly remembered the seafood platter he'd ordered from Groove Cities Finest Seafood. The restaurant had only been open for a year, and already it had won the hearts of all the residents of Groove City. Walking out of his office, Blyss noticed Beautii's light on and her door open. He made a mental note to turn her light off, and close her door before going back to his office. *Let me call and check on her now.* Blyss retrieved his phone from his pocket, and went straight to Beautii's contact.

"Hello, this is Beautii," she answered, bent over, looking in the refrigerator looking for something to eat.

Blyss stood in place at the door frame, with his eyes trained on Beautii's plump ass. Immediate words evaded him, as he inwardly wondered how he didn't know Beautii was still in the office.

Standing straight up, Beautii repeated. "Hello," then turned around, and damn near dropped her phone when she noticed Blyss standing in the door frame with a sexy smirk on his face. She'd done her best to avoid him for the sake of professionalism, but she'd conveniently gotten lost in reverie countless times since their last encounter. The way he spoke to her, the things he said, and the way he'd made her feel was every woman's dream. Her panties became soaked every time she thought about it.

"I thought you left for the day," Blyss licked his lips and said.

"Umm… yeah. That was the plan, but after viewing some of my deadlines, I decided to stay," Beautii stammered over her words.

"I can dig it," Blyss nodded. "This is Groove City. It never rains in Southern California. I've been here twenty plus years, and it hasn't happened yet. They predict this shit every year, and it never happens." Blyss nonchalantly explained.

"Those were my exact thoughts too. Of course, I just moved here, but I never heard of it raining here before."

"Welcome to the desert." Blyss joked, and they both laughed. "What you got for dinner?"

"I'll have to order something. I thought I had something in the fridge, but it's not there anymore." Beautii blew out a frustrated breath and replied.

"Was it some pasta and garlic bread?" Blyss asked, opening the refrigerator, and pulling out his food.

"Yes! How did you know?"

" 'Cause I threw it away earlier," Blyss said, as he walked deeper into the kitchen. "You eat seafood?"

"Yes, but why did you throw my food away?" Beautii crossed her arms, and asked.

"I don't like clutter," Blyss said, then pointed to the sign on the fridge that said. Anything in this refrigerator can be thrown away at any time. Blyss grabbed two plates from the cabinet. "I got enough to share, if you want some of my food," Blyss offered as he placed his food in the microwave to heat up.

"What kind of seafood you got?"

"Just some catfish, lobster, scallops, shrimp, crab cakes, seafood mac, and greens." Blyss said, turning back around to face her.

"Yes! Your food sounds and smells better than mine did anyway," Beautii smiled and accepted his offer.

Once all the food was warmed, Blyss washed his hands, then divided his platter evenly between them. At that moment, Blyss was glad he ordered two of everything. He served Beautii first, then went back to the counter to grab his food. Sitting his food on the table across from Beautii, he doubled back to pull out some veuve clicquot la grande dame and two wine glasses. Joining Beautii at the table, he poured them both a hefty glass of wine to go with their dinner.

"This is really good. Where did you get this from?" Beautii asked.

"Groove Cities Finest Seafood." Blyss answered after swallowing down the wine he'd just drank.

"Oh yeah. I've been meaning to try them out, but I always end up cooking my own food." Beautii shrugged. "Guess I get it from my mama."

"You like to cook, huh?"

"Yeah, I actually do."

"I bet you taste better than all this shit." Blyss chuckled. "I mean your food."

Beautii squeezed her thighs together tightly and shifted slightly in her seat to still her pulsating clit. Just the thought of Blyss' tongue swiveling around her clit had her struggling to hold her composure. Blyss was well aware of the weight of his word play, but he was still moving at her pace.

"I can do a little something in the kitchen." Beautii bashfully replied with a smile.

"Let me be the judge of that. When you gon' stop playin' and let me do a taste test?"

Beautii shifted again in her seat, then took a sip from her wine glass. "Whenever you wanna come by just let me know."

"Saturday."

"What do you have a taste for?"

"You on a platter, but I'll settle for whatever you feel like I deserve."

Beautii nodded her head. "Saturday. Can you be at my place at six o'clock for dinner, and maybe a movie afterwards?" Beautii asked, standing to her feet. Sitting down had become a task sitting across from Blyss.

"You runnin' from a nigga already, huh?" Blyss felt Beautii's energy, and wanted parts. Is this a date, Ms. Hamilton?"

"It's whatever you want it to be," Beautii winked. "I'm

gonna finish this food in my office, but thank you so much for sharing your food with me."

"I'm a gentleman, Beautii. I can feed you too," Blyss winked back. "I think I'ma go up there too. I'll be right behind you." Blyss replied, quickly picking up and throwing away the styrofoam containers and plastic bags.

Twenty minutes later, Blyss looked up once he heard the light sounds of Beautii's knuckles against his door. The way she stood there in her silk, penny colored wrap dress, all he wanted to do was unwrap her, and indulge in the gift between her slim thick thighs. Beautii's shape was a complete masterpiece that Blyss wanted to explore all night long into the morning, if she'd only let him. The look on Blyss' face told Beautii all she needed to know.

"You told me to come see you when I was ready right?" Beautii reminded Blyss of his words the last time they were together. "I'm ready now. Come get me."

Without delay, lightning flashed brightly, and lit up the sky like the fourth of July. Banging. Crashing. Thunder roared furiously from the sky. As sizzling electrifying lightning clapped and zipped across the night sky, causing the lights to shut down instantly. The clouds opened her mouth, and spat out big amounts of water at dangerous speeds. The high winds murmured through the thick windows of the office sounding like a swarm of buzzing, angry bees.

With little to no effort, Beautii made Blyss' heart race at dangerous levels. Though her presence was unexpected, Blyss' appreciated the thrill he received from being put on the spot. All his life he'd been an overachiever, and his performance on and off the job was top tier consistently. Sabrina Claudio's *Naked* played enticingly in the background, as Blyss' stood to his feet, and ambled slowly in Beautii's direction; drinking her in with his eyes as she stood there awaiting his arrival.

Unbuttoning his shirt, revealing his muscular chest adorned with tattoo's that made Beautii weak; they were so sexy. Stepping into Beautii's space, Blyss' lowered his head to the nape of her neck. The vibrant notes of her perfume wafted up his nose, and simultaneously aroused and got him high. Pressing both hands on the wall, and boring deep into her orbs; Blyss spoke in her left ear in between the tender kisses he delivered up and down the crease of her neck. "This is a one way street called the point of no return, you need to know what time it is before we proceed." Blyss used his tongue and dragged it up to the tip of her ear, then slightly bit down. "Do you trust me?"

"No woman should ever ride a man's wave until he's shown her he knows how to surf," she moaned unapologetically in his ear.

"What have I shown you?" Blyss curiously asked, as he untied Beautii's silk bow that kept her dress in place.

Beautii pulled Blyss' head back slightly, then replied. "That I can trust your frequency, and you won't hurt me." She couldn't take it anymore, she needed to feel his heavenly lips on hers again. It was as if they were breathing life into each other, and getting high at the same time. They'd turned into fiends, undoubtedly addicted to one another.

Blyss' heart lurched in his chest, his dick hardened as he sensed her vulnerability, and the sight of her surrenderance humbled him. Had him ready to explore an area he'd never opened himself to before; making love. Before Beautii walked into his life, he'd never entertained the thought. He wasn't a fan of trusting any woman with his heart. Blyss was a man in every facet of the definition, both literally and figuratively.

With ease, Beautii skillfully, yet gently stripped Blyss' layers as if she was peeling the skin back from a banana.

Comparable with the new stream of lightning that ripped through the sky, electricity raced down Beautii's spine, and caused her to kneel instinctively. Looking up at Blyss submissively, she asked. "Can I talk to him?"

The rising of Blyss' erection through his Tom Ford suit pants permitted Beautii to express herself freely. Reaching up, Beautii loosed his Cartier leather belt buckle, and released Blyss' thick, long, heavy pole. Beautii licked her lips, as her heartbeat hastened, and high-octane adrenaline rushed through her body. Slow and tenderly, Beautii slid her tongue up and down Blyss' shaft, stopping at the head of his thick mushroom-shaped head.

"Mmm, fuck Beautii," Blyss murmured, hardening even more at the feel of Beautii's warm breath and soft lips.

Without hesitation, Beautii widened her mouth, and slurped Blyss' dick in like a vacuum. Skillfully, she introduced Blyss' dick to the back of her throat. Up and down, she glided slowly, wetting his manhood with her saliva and passion.

"Stop," Blyss instructed, on the verge of his release. "Come here."

"Yes," Beautii answered, as she allowed her silk dress to stream down her body like a waterfall.

Stepping out of his shoes, pants, and briefs at the same time. Blyss pinned Beautii against the wall. Both breathing erratically, Blyss entered, and filled Beautii's pussy to the hilt. He left no vacancies, he was placed in her life to complete her.

"Mmmm... Ssss... Ohhh, Blyss!" Beautii's pussy choked and released his shaft repeatedly as she came on the first stroke.

"That's right. Let a nigga hear you scream." Blyss delivered long-strokes consistently to Beautii's sweet spot. "Drench that muthafucka," Blyss coached Beautii as he eased in and out of her with intense passion. Blyss' endeavor was to extensively explore every inch of Beautii's pussy. Blyss' had studied Beautii's physique from afar for two years. He became a student, as her body trained him, and divulged the blueprint willingly as he pleased her with A1-certified dick.

Slowly, he eased out of her once he felt her body semi relax. Blyss was nowhere near done working her body over. He unbuttoned his shirt, reached forward to unsnap Beautii's bra, then slid her straps down her arms. Kneeling down in front of Beautii, he leaned forward and took a long sniff of her pussy. Beautii was a live aphrodisiac, Blyss realized once his sober mind became instantly intoxicated.

As the thunder rolled through the sky, thick droplets of rain sprayed the window like bullets; as Beautii threw her head back in pleasure. Blyss had commenced to beating Beautii's pussy into submission with the vicious swipes to her clit that left her weak in the knees. With one hand, Blyss supported her stance. With the other, he spread her lower lips further apart and continued to lay down his whip appeal. It was better than love, and sweet as can be.

As if in tune with the weather outside, bolts of pleasure shot down Beautii's spine at the sound of lightning clanking in the sky before hitting the ground. "Blyss!" Beautii sang his name soprano style. The harmony was so sweet, it sent electric signals to Blyss' dick; causing it to jolt and harden at the pleasant sound of Beautii's voice.

Looking up at the faint view of Beautii's eyes. "Bring that ass here," Blyss commanded, then smacked Beautii's ass. The sound mimicked the clapping sound that shot through the sky.

Obeying his command, Beautii sashayed over to the window pane beside Blyss' desk. With her legs parted, back arched, and her hands positioned flat on top of the flat surface; Beautii seductively moved her ass around in a circle as she awaited Blyss' entrance.

Turned on by the tropical scenery, and thrill of the slight danger of what they were doing; Blyss plunged deep inside her wetness without thinking twice. Infinite pleasure. Blyss had delved into an oasis of joy he never knew existed as he explored the depth of Beautii's haven. *Fuckin' Paradise!* Blyss thought as he reached up to pinch himself. *Am I dead?* Blyss questioned himself in disbelief. Blyss watched a thin layer of sweat mist atop of her melanated skin like a vapor from convectional rainfall. Looking down, Blyss admired the sight of Beautii's ass crashing against his pelvis. Perfection was something he'd never achieved during the process of sex with any woman, but with Beautii it was majestic. Elevated.

Clutching her love handles tightly, Blyss hit a spot inside of Beautii that had him floating in and out of consciousness. His thighs locked in place as electric waves turned into kinetic energy, and flowed intrinsically through Blyss' body and shot through Beautii's spine. Blyss blasted inside of Beautii, as she met her third climax.

# CHAPTER EIGHT

## BEAUTII HAMILTON

*"All those days and lonely nights have finally gone away. I never thought the day would come, that we'd be more than friends. You made me smile, when I was down. You turned my world around. The way you give me love feels so right..."*

Still on a Blyss infused high from the night before, Beautii embraced the fact that she was able to hibernate, and work from home. There was no doubt in her mind after she encountered Blyss Valentino, his dick was simply dipped in crack. Sitting in front of her Apple computer screen in her home office, Beautii felt like she had a secret, and she just couldn't get situated until she told it. Grabbing her phone off her mahogany wood desk, she immediately silenced Toni Braxton's *I Love Me Some Him*, and connected her bluetooth after pressing Fayth's contact.

"Hey Sis!" Fayth answered on the third ring. "I heard about that storm that hit Groove City last night. I kept trying to call you, but I couldn't get through. I was worried sick." Fayth rambled on.

Beautii pressed the button for facetime and waited for Fayth to accept it before she replied. The instant she saw Fayth's face, she gleamed with genuine joy. "Hey Pooh!" Beautii grinned. "It stormed pretty bad last night, but I was in good hands. I mean... I was alright." Beautii said, then bit down on her bottom lip.

"Uhn uhn, hoe. Who got you over there glowing like that? Let me find out, you don' went to Groove City, and got you some mandingo!" Fayth said, sliding to the edge of her seat, and pursing her lips close to the screen.

Beautii hollered. "Babyyy, let me tell you about, Mr. Blyss Valentino!"

"Bitch, I know you lyin'... Shut the front door!"

"When have you ever known me to lie about something like this?"

"Damnnnn... That man is a complete masterpiece, and the total package." Fayth stated the obvious. "Now that's the nigga you need to build with! I'm so proud of you, sis."

"Slow down, now. It was only one night of pleasure. We haven't discussed a relationship, or anything of that nature. It just happened last night after we had dinner and a few drinks."

"Oh, and ya pussy just accidentally slid down his dick? You betta spill the tea before I hop on a flight. Stop playing."

"Hol' up! Is that a passion mark I see on your neck?" Beautii curiously pressed, as soon as her eyes landed on a big red circle just above Fayth's collar bone.

Fayth gushed, looked away from the phone, and covered her mouth.

"What's his name?" Beautii asked.

"Tyson Dubois," Fayth revealed.

Beautii took a moment to make the connection. Shen knew she'd heard that name before. Then it dawned on her. "Tyson

Dubois! He works for Trenton Dubois law firm in Chicago?" Beautii quizzed.

"Yes. Tyson is Trenton's son," Fayth confirmed.

"What?! Why the hell didn't I know anything about this before now? How?"

"Chillee... I met him at Langston and Suks while we were waiting for you and Mr. Valentino to arrive with dad."

"Oh, so we're holding secrets now?"

"I wouldn't say all that. I mean in all honesty, it really wasn't that much to tell. We hadn't had a conversation or anything. I just got his number when I came out of the ladies room, then went back to the table to wait with mom." Fayth told Beautii truthfully, and shrugged.

"Well, now it's a whole lot to tell with that big ass hickey on your neck." Beautii said, with widened eyes.

"Listennn... working with Attorney Stith has been nothing short of amazing. I've learned so much from her. I had to take on a case a few weeks ago that required me to reach out to his father. Since he was unable to fit me in his schedule, he referred me to his son, Tyson. How ironic is that?"

"Girl, so how did y'all end up in bed together?" Beautii impatiently pressed for more details.

"His house. His bed. His pipe. Hunni, it was all out of this world." Fayth laughed. "I ended up flying to Chicago due to the sensitivity of the case. It wasn't safe to discuss over the phone. Tyson ended up inviting me to his house, and after putting our heads together, time just seemed to fly by. When I looked at the clock it was after midnight. We'd had a few drinks, and we'd been flirting off and on throughout the day. One thing led to another, and boom." Fayth gave the condensed version of the story.

"Was it worth it?"

"Yes ma'am!" Fayth exclaimed. "Sis, this is him beeping in on the other line. Can I call you right back?"

"Yeah, Yeah. Go ahead, I'll talk to you later."

"You better answer the phone when I call too. I still wanna hear about you and Blyss."

"Okay, sis." Beautii replied before ending the call. The music started back up automatically, as pensive thoughts of Blyss took up residence in her mind. The task of eluding her mental state from constant thoughts of Blyss seemed wildly unreasonable; absurd even. It had taken Beautii two years to detox her contaminated soul from the residue Bilaal left behind. Now that she'd unexpectedly given herself to Blyss, she couldn't help but think about how this changed everything. *God, what have I done? I should have just gone home. This is all my fault.*

Beautii blamed herself and got stuck in a warp of pessimistic thoughts. She'd worked hard to become the woman she was, and was terrified of losing it all for a night of pleasure. The vibrations against her desk, yanked her mind out of the rabbit hole it was going down. The mere sight of Blyss' name lit up on her phone screen had her stomach in knots. Extreme apprehension filled her gut as she held her phone and watched it ring. She took in a deep breath and released it loudly when Blyss hung up. A few seconds later, Blyss called back again. *Oh my God, what if it's about business. See, this is why I can't be doin' this type of shit.* Beautii shook herself quickly, then answered the phone.

"Hello, this is Beautii Hamilton," Beautii used the most professional voice she could muster up.

Blyss cracked up laughing as soon as he heard Beautii's voice. "Oh, this what we doin'? We back to the formal greetings?" Blyss asked, already sensing her reluctance about how to move forward after what had transpired between them.

"I... I just-"

"Need to relax like you did last night. Nigga can't even focus on work after what we did." Blyss honestly admitted. "It's your world, Beautii. All a nigga need to know is where I fit inside your life, 'cause you for damn sure changed mine."

"This is all happening so fast, Blyss. I'm honestly still trying to process it all."

"Let me take you out tomorrow night around eight. We can process, unpack, and digest it together."

"I don't even know what to say."

"Say yes, baby." Blyss knew he was coming on strong, but he needed Beautii to know he wasn't playing games in his pursuit of her.

"Yes," Beautii instinctively responded the same way she had when Blyss commanded her body. They both had each other's minds gone.

"We'll all be working from home for the rest of this week. There's a few electrical issues that need to be looked at. Everything will be back up and running by Monday." Blyss informed Beautii before disconnecting their call.

"I'll see you tomorrow, Mr. Valentino."

"You will. But, keep talking to me like that... you gon' fuck around and see me today."

Beautii easily fell into a short fit of laughter. The energy had always been easy between the duo, and Beautii appreciated the reminder. Blyss was the epitome of newness of life wrapped in one fine ass package. *Blyss Valentino.* Saying his name in her mind made her body tremble. Pushing back from her desk, she decided to take a break because she couldn't focus anyway.

Dressed in a nude designer dress, Beautii stood in front of her massive floor to ceiling mirror in her bedroom admiring her light makeup as she combed down her long wrap. She didn't know what to expect, but she hadn't eaten all day. Approving her finished look, Beautii put a little more lipstick on, then tossed it in her purse. Before turning off the lights, Beautii sprayed herself with *Emporio Armani Diamonds Intense*, then pressed play on her Spotify Oasis playlist, and hit repeat. As she made her way down the stairs, her doorbell rang.

"Just a minute," Beautii announced, looking up at the clock. *Umm, he's on time,* Beautii duly noted. Instantly, she noticed as soon as she opened the door, a box of peach and ivory colored roses in a black *Venus ET Fleur* box, and a light blue gift bag from Tiffany & Co. Beautii was convinced that Blyss majored in snatching her breath away. It wasn't so much the gifts he carried, but it was the giver. His aura. His presence. The way Beautii immediately longed to be cocooned in the security of his arms. *Am I dreaming?*

Dapper in a crisp black button down, paired with crystal black onyx cufflinks, Blyss wore gray slacks. Feet clad with black designer loafers. Beautii was moved to silence as her eyes scanned his physique. Blyss stayed fly everyday, so Beautii expected nothing less.

"You did all this for me?" Blyss asked, breaking the silence as he bore into Beautii's eyes with purpose. "Your parents gave you the right name, 'cause God knows He blessed you with rare beauty." Blyss complimented, while handing Beautii the gifts he bought for her.

"Thank you," she replied. "Please step in for a moment, I

need to grab my purse, my phone and keys." Beautii stepped back and invited, as she opened the door wider for Blyss to come in. After closing the door, Beautii quickly made her way to the half bathroom that was located a few steps beyond the living room. Nervously, she stood in the mirror to make sure she matched Blyss' fly.

Without warning, Blyss walked in the bathroom, and stood behind her. "Don't change, or fix nothing. You're perfect as you are." Blyss confirmed, then kissed the back of her head. "Come on, we have reservations."

"Thank you," Beautii took Blyss' word for it, as she turned the light off and followed his lead. She grabbed her purse off of the sofa table that was situated behind her couch, checked to make sure she had her phone and keys, then secured her house as she and Blyss walked out together.

The duo walked side by side to Blyss' white S680 Maybach. Pressing the button on his key fob, Blyss opened the door for Beautii, and waited until she snapped her seatbelt to close the door. As he walked around to the driver side of the car, he halted in place to look around. Something felt off to him, but he couldn't put his finger on it. Ignoring his gut, Blyss opened the door and joined Beautii in his car. "You ready?" Blyss looked over and asked Beautii before backing out.

"Yes, I'm ready." Beautii rubbed her lips together, then smiled warmly. The sound of Phora's *Faithful* spilled tastefully through the speakers.

Blyss reached over the console for Beautii's hand, then intertwined his fingers with hers. Beautii felt seen. With everything in her, she questioned how Blyss knew her. How he knew to play this song, revealing the sentiments of her heart. She knew she was a good woman, and had all it took to be any man's most prized possession. However, she had come up short down the line. She had all the love she could contain on the inside of her, but no one real to understand, and share with. Tightening his grip, Blyss glanced over at Beautii, then refocused his attention on the road. No words were necessary in that moment, he felt her spirit, and that was enough for her.

*Thirty Minutes Later…*

Opening Beautii's door and helping her out of the car, they walked hand in hand into the Oasis Art Gallery. Beautii looked around, amazed by a myriad of diverse art pieces. It was so much to take in at once, but she loved the space she'd just entered. Everything from wall art to hand casting-heirloom pieces.

"All of this art is astonishing. I love it all." Beautii was in awe of every creation her eyes connected with.

"Yea, it is pretty dope," Blyss agreed. "Come with me, I wanna show you something, then we can come back down here." Blyss said, leading the way towards the elevators.

"Oh my God, there's more?" Beautii was amazed by what she saw already. The thought of more added on seemed like too much. She'd never been on a date like this before. In times past, she was the one who always had to do all the planning, and nothing was a surprise to her. To say this was a pleasant surprise would be an extreme understatement. Overwhelmed with joy was more like it.

Stepping on the elevator, Blyss hit the button for the eleventh floor which had to be the roof, Beautii assumed because there were no other floors higher. As soon as the elevator opened, Beautii covered her mouth with both hands in utter shock. Blyss had peach and black rose petals spread on top of an ivory colored carpet, leading the path to a table set for two in the middle of the roof as soon as they stepped off the elevator. The mix of candles, overview of the city, and the savory smell of food set the tone for a romantic evening. Beautii wasn't a hard woman to please, and Blyss was setting a new bar.

"You like it?" Blyss sincerely asked.

"Do I like it? Tuh! I love all of this. Thank you so much, Blyss." Beautii wrapped her arms around his neck, and kissed his cheek. "I can't believe you went through all this trouble."

"I've seen and done a lot in this life, Beautii. I've experienced the best and worst of both worlds." Blyss looked out at the dimly lit buildings that were so far away, yet seemed as if they could be touched by simply reaching out. "I've never met a woman like you. Never thought a woman could be an asset to my life, and make me feel so…" Blyss paused a moment. "Open. I've known since the day you walked into my office that there was an immense significance about you. What unfolded between us the other night only solidified the fact that I've been harshly depriving myself of the one thing missing in my life. So, yea… make no mistake about it, a nigga checkin' for you, and I ain't stoppin' til your last name becomes Valentino."

If there was ever a time Beautii was uncertain, it was non-existent when it came to Blyss. The abundance of strength, security, and assurance he exuded, exposed Beautii to an oasis of possibilities. She felt an oasis of newness begging to be released, if only she'd tap into unknown territory, and trust the winds to flow in her favor. Trust that everything she'd been manifesting for the last two years was ready to spring forth.

"I guess this is just the tip of the iceberg, huh?"

"Just the tip, baby. I won't promise you the world, 'cause together we have the power, ability, and funds to create whatever world we want." Blyss promised her. "Right now, all I wanna do is feed you, talk, and have a good time. Is that alright?"

Beautii nodded, and watched as Blyss moved the chair to the space next to him. "I hope you don't mind. I need you closer to me."

"Good evening, Mr. Valentino. My name is Calvin, and I'll be your server for the night." Calvin nodded his head in Beautii's direction, then continued to talk to Blyss. "Tonight, we'll be serving seared lamb tips, garlic mashed potatoes, and cabbage. We also have a nice sweet red wine that quickly became a fan favorite. Will this be all for you two tonight?" Calvin asked, while his twin brother Curtis sat their entrees down in front of them.

"Yes, this looks amazing," Beautii answered with her signature smile, bringing more light into the space they were sitting in.

Blyss had already selected their meal when he made reservations. Therefore, he wasted no time digging in after drinking some of his wine.

"Why are you doing all of this?" Beautii needed to know Blyss' intentions.

"'Cause I wanted to look at you without being disturbed."

"Interesting."

"That you are. I been tryna figure out how your fine ass got me out of my element." Blyss divulged honestly. Being in Beautii's presence was something like a divine experience. She made him feel celestial, he'd gotten so high the other night; he dreaded coming back down to deal with the natural elements of realistic life.

Beautii blushed.. "And, how'd I do that exactly?"

"Shit, you tell me." Blyss shot back. In his mind Beautii had exceeded the effects of fentanyl. People died from taking one hit, but with Beautii; Blyss didn't give a damn, one touch from her would be enough to resuscitate him.

There was so much Beautii wanted to say, so many questions she wanted to ask, but the deeper she looked into Blyss' eyes; she found all the answers she needed. Instead of offering an explanation, Beautii took a small bite of her lamb tip. "This is really tasty."

"Umhmm. You want some dessert after this?"

"Is this a trick question?"

"Not at all."

"Actually, I prefer to eat snickers if I eat anything sweet. I'm not really into cakes or pies."

Blyss chuckled. "Oh yea? I must admit, I love banana pudding, and oatmeal cream pies."

"I make the best banana pudding. I'll have to make you some one day."

"Oh, you already made me a believer. Your mom made sure she packed me some of the banana pudding you made when I came by there. It was nothing compared to the homemade flavor you coated my tongue with though."

Impenitently, Beautii felt her gut tense as evocative memories of their rendezvous knocked at her frontal cortex, causing her heart to overflow with hysteria. Blyss was such a transparent man. Bold. Vigilant. He was always on point, and he won at everything he did simply because he didn't play.

"Tell me something," Blyss said. "Are you done pinching marbles?"

"I'm not sure that I follow?"

"Are you done fuckin' with that lame ass nigga, Billy? I need to know, 'cause the shit I have planned for us gon' require you to be all in."

Beautii laughed. "Who the hell is Billy? I swear, you childish for that comment." Beautii continued to laugh.

Blyss shrugged. "Whatever the hell that soft ass nigga name is. Let me know what's up? I'm tryna make history with you by my side."

Beautii squinted her eyes, pushed her plate back, then took a sip of her wine. "You sure this is what you want? I can't afford to play no games with my heart."

"Check this out, beautiful. When a man is blessed to find a rare diamond in a world full of cubic zirconia, he'd be a fool to take it for granted. He'd be insane to take a chance on losing it. Neglect is a punishment only a lesser man with no understanding would inflict. A real man knows when he's found the missing part of his life. A real man facilitates so much wealth and wisdom, he's able to pour into his woman without depleting himself," Blyss explained. "Now, you're an intelligent woman, and you see extremely well. Tell me what kind of man you take me as?"

The answer was indubitably clear. "You're a wise man," Beautii replied. "Exceptionally wise to recognize when you're in the company of a real woman, and to acknowledge the asset I can be to you professionally and personally. What I'm not clear on, is what exactly you're asking me right now. I never took you as a man to beat around the bush. You're a go-getter."

"I want you to be my woman, Beautii? Nigga ain't tryna have casual sex with you. I want all of you."

Beautii smiled. "I like how that sounds. I believe I can handle that. I want you too."

Drinking the last of his wine, Blyss emerged from his chair. Walking over to the ledge, he looked over the city, then sat back on the oversized, plush chair situated near the ledge. With a raised brow, and deep eye contact, Blyss chucked his head; pointing towards his lap. Beautii favorably obliged his request without hesitation. Slowly, she took seductive strides towards Blyss, then straddled him. Her dress that reached just below the tip of her middle finger when she stood, barely covered her plump, round ass. The bulge between Blyss' legs ignited the flow of her essence through the thin, sheer panties she wore that scarcely served as a mild barrier, and covered her sacred oasis.

Blyss naturally reached forward and grabbed a handful of Beautii's ass in the palm of his hands, then gave it a firm squeeze. Their lips hugged each other as if they were long lost friends, and they'd been deprived from each other for over a complete decade. Like a deer thirsting for water, Blyss' dick yearned to be engulfed in Beautii's wondrous stream. Empowered. Addicted. Fascinated. Blyss swore Beautii had him under some kind of hypnosis. The way Beautii's pussy gripped his dick, had him wondering what the hell he'd been doing all his life. Blyss lost his virginity at fifteen years old, he was lowkey pissed that he'd spent over three decades emotionlessly fucking women. Deprived. Even though he knew he'd deprived himself, he was elated to start a transparent journey with Beautii. Simultaneously, their chests heaved and their hearts raced as they anticipated the inevitable.

"Fuck," Blyss rasped in Beautii's ear. "You must want a nigga to massage that pussy again? Fill you up, and make you scream my name," Blyss muttered, then slid Beautii's panties to the side.

Slightly raising up, she allowed Blyss to free his manhood. Greedily, Beautii's pussy welcomed him in as she sat back down. Grinding back and forth, then rotating her hips in circular motions, she rode Blyss' wave like a pro.

Grabbing the bent part of Beautii's knees, Blyss created slight friction as he plunged deeper inside Beautii's oasis.

"Beautii," Blyss groaned. "You gon' make a nigga go insane inside this pussy."

"That's what I want, baby. Lose yourself in this pussy, it belongs to you now." Beautii moaned, as she willingly gave up her rights to Blyss. She surrendered. Agreed to the exchange that had already taken place between them.

"Release baby," Beautii sexily commanded. "Give it to me."

"Ahh, fuck, Beautii." Blyss released an impenitent nut inside of her.

Wrapped tight in each other's arms, the world around them spun, but they were frozen in the moment. Beautii nurtured Blyss, and Blyss strengthened and cocooned Beautii as his dick pulsed inside her walls.

One Hour Later…

Paradise. If there was one word to express and describe what Beautii was experiencing, paradise was the best word she could think of. Candidly, having sex on top of the world was enough to give Beautii a glimpse of what heaven looked, sounded, and felt like at night; she wanted to visit frequently. It was a memory that would be forever etched in her mind. Walking out of the ladies room. Beautii rejoined Blyss, as he waited for her out in the broad hallway of the establishment.

If the look of appreciation and admiration had a face, it would look exactly like Blyss. He studied the way Beautii walked with confidence when she was in a professional setting, and appreciated the way she strutted sexily when she was in his presence. He listened to her speak for two years, so he knew when she was nervous, she constantly smoothed out invisible wrinkles in her clothes. When Blyss peeped Beautii walking out of the bathroom smoothing her hands down the sides of her dress, he realized how she'd already started her process of overthinking what was budding between them.

"He-"

Beautii's words were terminated as soon as she came within arms reach of Blyss. He pulled her gently into his embrace, then delicately pressed his lips into hers. "I don't regret shit about what we've done," Blyss spoke into Beautii's mouth. "I'm not ashamed of you, and I don't plan on creepin' around with you. We belong together, baby. Everything about us makes sense in every way. Don't you agree?" Blyss quizzed, gazing deep into Beautii's eyes.

"Yes," Beautii whispered, as she softly caressed the right side of Blyss' face.

"Come here," Blyss said, as if she wasn't already close enough. After sharing another passionate kiss, Blyss stepped back and regained his composure. "I have another surprise for you." Side by side, hands clasped, Beautii and Blyss made their way down to the end of the hallway.

"Blyss Valentino… I see you made it here after all," the hand casting instructor greeted as the duo walked through the last door on the right side of the hall.

"Yea man, just wanted to do something nice and meaningful with my lady."

"Well, hello there. My name is Julez," the instructor introduced himself. "It's nice to meet you."

"Likewise. My name is Beautii." She smiled then reached forward to shake Julez' hand.

"You've got a winner on your hands here," Julez complimented and directed his comment to Blyss.

"Already," Blyss replied, while Beautii took the liberty of looking around at some of the other hand-casting pieces that were on display around the room.

"Oh my God, this one is so beautiful," Beautii lifted the

hand-piece up and admired it. "How much is this? I'd like to purchase this, and sit it in my living room." Beautii asked, still mesmerized by all the fine art she was surrounded by.

"The pieces that you're looking at are personal for me, so they're not for sale; only display. But, if the piece you're holding is something you really want, I can show you and Blyss how to make it." Julez assured.

"Yes, I'd love that. Blyss, do you wanna make this with me?" Beautii held up what Julez had labeled as, *The Lingering Touch Sculpture.* It was a timeless, perfect, and elegant accent piece. Suitable for a variety of decorating themes in home or office settings.

"Ahh, yes. This resin sculpture depicts two hands clinging together in a lingering embrace. I see you have a sharp eye for classics. I can appreciate that." Julez perceived. "The bronze finish has light bronze and golden highlights. Very intriguing piece that you'll have a chance to choose rather you'd prefer a black or brown base for."

"This is the best date I've ever been on in my life," Beautii revealed. Thank you so much for bringing me here, Blyss."

"I figured you'd like something like this." Blyss winked, then sat down at the wooden table, while Julez went to gather everything they'd need to get the process started.

"How'd you figure that?" Beautii quizzed.

" 'Cause you always talkin' 'bout how you loathe doing the same shit all the time. Hand-casting ain't something everybody knows about, much less entertaining the train of thought that would lead them to check into it. Shit, people are more privy to pottery than they are to hand casting. And, even with that, people ain't really jumpin' at the opportunity to make a vase or a bowl." Blyss replied, leaving very little room for rebuttal, mainly because he was telling the truth.

While the duo occupied their time together, a heap of

turbulence lurked in the heart of Bilaal. The hotel building that was bilateral to Oasis Art Gallery gave Bilaal front row seats to the show Beautii and Blyss had put on, unaware of anyone watching them.

*I'ma get my bitch back, and I don't give a fuck who gotta die in the process. If it kills me, then I'll die for a good cause. Love.* Bilaal thought as he contemplated his next move. He'd been watching Beautii ever since the day he'd seen her at Langston & Suks.

## CHAPTER NINE

### BILAAL HARRIS

*"Oh, tell me now. Is you tryna break me, or you tryna make me something better off? For shit that I painted, for shit that they see. For shit that I live, and the things that I breathe. They don't want me to succeed, I still ain't make it out. I see it all in my dreams..."*

*I*n the still of the night, Bilaal sat down on the side of his bed, smoked a blunt, and vibed with YoungBoy's *Break or Make Me*. There was something about the words of this song that uncovered the essence of how he truly felt. He'd been through a lot of hell in his life, but Beautii; she was his slice of heaven. Like the desert needing the rain, Bilaal found it impossible to overcome the insurmountable feeling of needing Beautii back in his life. He closed his eyes and thought back to the good times they shared. Bilaal hoped and prayed for the restoration of those days.

 Reaching over to his nightstand, Bilaal picked up his phone and scrolled to the pictures he had saved of Beautii and himself when they were on good terms. Despite his beliefs of living in the present, Beautii's absence forced him to remain stuck in the past. Reminiscing on the good days was something that inevitably became a habit he reluctantly inhabited the day he realized Beautii was serious about leaving him. Bilaal easily became mesmerized as he admired everything about Beautii. From her long mane that streamed from her roots down past the center of her back, her smooth brown skin that always glowed, to the gray contacts that covered her mesmerizing chestnut-colored eyes. No matter how many times Bilaal told her that she didn't need embellishments, she still did extra from time to time. Naturally, Beautii was goddess-like in Bilaal's eyes, he just wished she could see herself from his perspective. Women paid for curves that Beautii was born with, they prayed their enhancements made them look half as good.

    Taking another toke from his blunt, Bilaal lazily dragged his finger across the screen of his cell phone when Willow's name appeared.

    "Yuh," Bilaal answered, blowing out a cloud of smoke.

    "Did you forget what today was?" Willow quizzed, beyond irritated.

    "Whatever it is, it must not be that important," Bilaal snickered and dismissed.

    "If it ain't about Beautii, it ain't important? You are so foul Bilaal, I swear! You movin' real bogus. We had a life before running into your precious Beautii. Now you act like you can't think past her!" Willow fumed on the other end of the phone.

    "Fuck you mean, yo? You been on my line talkin' shit for the last two minutes, and still haven't said what the fuck you want!"

    "My doctor appointment is today. You promised you'd

never miss any of my doctor's appointments, and that our kids would always come first." Willow shook her head and cried. "You promised me you wouldn't leave me hanging with two kids by myself."

Bilaal let out an exasperated sigh. "Come on man, chill with all that cryin' shit. I forgot about the appointment, and now I got some otha shit I gotta carry out today. It's just one appointment, Willow, damn. Cut me some slack. I'll be there for the next one."

"Ain't no next one, Bilaal! This is the last one. I'm due to have our daughter any day now, or have you forgot about that? I mean since ya mindset so fucked up now."

"Miss me with this bullshit, Willow. I just told yo ass I can't make it today. I'll be there for the birth of my seed. The fuck else you want from a nigga? We not together, I'on owe yo' ass shit!"

"Son of a bitch, you owe me a whole fuckin' lot! You always -"

CLICK...

Past the point of aggravation, Bilaal hung up on Willow. *This shit is beyond me. This bitch is crazy as hell.* Bilaal concluded, as he finished smoking his blunt. Bilaal shook his head, frustrated with himself, annoyed by the pending circumstances he had created. Willow wasn't a bad woman, she just fell for a man who was in love with another woman; and didn't know it. She fell for a man who'd filled her head with false truths and no real intention. Bilaal had walked into Willow's life with one mission, one motive, and one thought; to fuck her silly. He'd done that thinking he'd hit once and be out, but her snatch had a hold on him. Bilaal was most comfortable in the fast lane, and he thrived living the street life. That is, until it all caught up with him. By the time he snapped back into reality, he'd lost everything.

Bilaal lived in a prison of his own problems, and lacked any real solutions for himself, much less Willow, or his kids for that matter. In his mind, everything had to take a backseat until he found his happy place. Until he was content with his life. Many people would call this way of thinking selfish as hell, and to some degree it is. However, it was Bilaal's reality. He didn't know how to make himself happy, yet in his own way, he'd tried to make everyone around complete. His conclusion was the necessity of his own happiness first. There was no way he was going to keep being a dream come true to other people, while his dreams were constantly deferred.

*Beautii.* Bilaal's spirit called to her through the darkness. She was his dream woman. Everything he needed, she possessed, and surpassed all he could ever desire.

*The right thing at the wrong time, is undoubtedly the wrong thing, baby. I know you care for that woman, but if you can't do right by her, please leave her alone. If you don't listen to me, you're gonna wish you did. If you don't listen, your heart is gonna bleed something serious one day. Just may be your demise.*

The words of Bilaal's grandma Sarah replayed in his mind as tears slid down his face. Bilaal wasn't an emotional man, but he was living proof of how the same thing that makes you laugh, will make you cry.

"I gotta get her back. I need her." Bilaal whispered to himself.

Drastic times call for drastic measures. Bilaal wasn't sure who originated this quote, but he knew there was no time like the present. If he ever stood a chance at getting Beautii back, he needed to move swiftly. He needed to do something extreme to simultaneously gain her attention, and woo her. There was no extreme action Bilaal wouldn't walk out to fulfill his desires to build something fresh with Beautii.

Bilaal wasn't the type to go with the flow, he specialized in interrupting shit, and creating his own flow. He called Beautii's job, and made an appointment under a false alias. Had he given his real name there was no way he would have made it past the receptionist. Bilaal had observed and done his homework concerning Beautii's schedule, and had it down to a science. There were some days that were hectic, but those days were Tuesday and Wednesday. Bilaal decided Monday was the best day to come in.

"Good morning, and welcome to Regal Valentino Law Office. How may we serve you today?" Jillian greeted.

"Good morning. My name is Bi… DeMarcus Benson. I have an eight o'clock appointment with Ms. Beautii Hamilton this morning.

Jillian's fingertips rhythmically swayed swiftly across the keyboard. "Alright, I've got you all pulled up. Can I get you to look over this paper, and sign at the bottom once you're done please?" Jillian grabbed a clipboard and passed it forward. Once checked in, Jillian called Beautii to let her know her eight o'clock appointment with DeMarcus Benson had arrived. Beautii instructed her to send him up to her office.

Approximately five minutes later, Bilaal had made it to Beautii's office. She wasn't seated behind her desk, but he knew she was there. He knew he was in the right office because everywhere Beautii went, she made her mark. The way she'd decorated her office peach and black, with hints of gold and silver was a dead give away; not to mention her distinct scent. Bilaal knew her scent better than he knew his own. Assuming she'd taken a bathroom break, he took the liberty of taking a seat and waiting for her to return.

"How did you get up here?" Beautii announced as soon as she saw Bilaal sitting in her office. She didn't need him to turn around to know it was him.

Raising from his seat to face her, Bilaal raised his hands in protest. "I'm just here to talk to you, baby. I don't wanna cause a scene. I swear a nigga don't want no problems."

"This is my job. Bilaal," Beautii shook her head in disbelief, on the verge of tears. "How dare you bring your bullshit to my job? I told you already that I was done with your ass. Why can't you get the shit through your thick ass skull?" Beautii yelled in a hushed tone.

"Just chill and let me holla at you for a minute," Bilaal begged.

"No! You need to get the fuck out of here before I call security." Beautii crossed her arms, and demanded.

Dropping to his knees in front of Beautii, Bilaal was left with no alternative but to plead. "Beautii please, baby. You got me out here all fucked up. Don't leave me like this, not again. Give me a chance to prove I can be a better man. Let me show you I've changed for you. All that otha shit a nigga was on before, I gave up for you. I left Willow and I'm out the streets completely," Bilaal told a half truth.

Fed up once again with all Bilaal's theatrics. "You, you, you. It's always all about you. What you want. What you need. How you feel. What you gave up." Beautii laughed factitiously. "You haven't changed at all, Bilaal. You still the same arrogant, bold, selfish man who refuses to take accountability for the fuck up's and damages you cause other people. Who hurt you?" Beautii asked, and was met with silence. The accountability Beautii demanded Bilaal to own, felt like an attack for several reasons. No one had ever called him out on his shit the way Beautii had, Bilaal still wasn't ready to acknowledge how his behavior dismantled the hearts of everyone who tried to love him.

"Just talk to me, and give me a chance to explain myself. I'll do whatever you want me to do. Just be with me. Open your heart to me again, and trust me not to hurt you." Bilaal humbled himself and continued to beg.

"I can't do this with you again. I'm-"

"Don't you dare part your lips to say that fucked up shit. I'll kill that nigga if you speak his name in my presence." Bilaal aggressively spat, heart filled with malice, despair, and jealousy. No matter how much he loved and wanted the best for Beautii, he didn't have what it took to sit back and watch Beautii be happy with another man. He'd die first.

"You gotta let me go, Bilaal. You gotta figure out how to resurrect the deep pain within you, and give it some place to exist outside of you. Put it in the music you create on your down time, devour it by building brighter connections with people you meet in the future," Beautii shook her head. "Your body is not a coffin for pain to be buried in. You need to see a therapist. Let them guide you through your healing and real freedom. What you're seeking is beyond me. I can't be your scapegoat, and I refuse to lend my light to you again. I'm not a storage bin for dead weight."

"Beautii," Blyss called out as soon as he stepped out of his office. "Beautii, you good? I heard yelling and…" Blyss inquired, as he stepped up and cocooned her protectively from behind. He stopped talking once his eyes landed on Bilaal down on his knees holding an engagement ring up towards Beautii. Looking back and forth between Beautii and Bilaal, he asked. "What's going on here?"

"Marry me, Beautii. I'll comply with whatever you require. I know I deserve to be cast to the side, and forgotten about. Don't do me like that, baby. Don't give me what I deserve. Just love me, Beautii. Love me like you always have, but a nigga was to blind to see. I see it now with more clarity than ever before. Let me love you back this time the way I should have all along."

Backing up further into Blyss' embrace, Beautii shook her head side to side, and allowed Blyss to gently kiss the side of her neck. "While you were taking time to realize what you took for granted, I was busy healing and becoming the best version of myself, so I could appreciate the new beginning God gave me. I don't love you anymore, Bilaal. I'm happy with Blyss, so please just walk away, and let me have what I deserve."

Rising to his feet, Bilaal replied. "Fuck all that shit you just said, Beautii. You don't mean that shit. How the fuck you so happy with this nigga, and ya pussy still fresh on my fuckin' tongue? Fuck on with that shit."

"Hol' up bitch ass, nigga. What you won't ever do, is come in my establishment, or anywhere I'm at and disrespect my woman. Whatever your grievances are, they don't mean shit here. If you had taken care of business the first time around, you would've never let a gem like Beautti slip from your grasp. But, you'z a lil' boy still tryna figure out where you fit in this world. Unlike you, I created my own, and muthafuckas eat because of the wealth I've generated. Now leave peacefully, or you can be escorted out." Blyss tightened his grip around Beautii's waist territorially. Letting her know she was still in a safe place without speaking one word to her.

"Pus' ass nigga! You got me fucked up! Your days are numbered, mark my words." Bilaal threatened Blyss.

The abysmal storm that brewed in the background of Blyss' eyes was impossible to overlook. Gently moving Beautii behind him, Blyss did his best to remain calm. Blyss saw beyond the obvious, and pulled Bilaal's hoe card. "Youz a bitch just like your father, the devil. You like doing shit to be seen, 'cause you didn't get enough attention when you grew up. Me on the other hand, I let muthafuckas like you feel me. See, I take after my father, God. I don't make threats, I keep my promises.

Beautii turned around and wrapped delicate arms around Blyss, and laid her head on his chest. "Thank you for coming to check on me babe. You always seem to know when I need you."

"I got you. Always and forever." Blyss promised, never taking his eyes off of Bilaal as he exited Beautii's office. "Make sure he leaves quietly," Blyss turned and instructed his personal security, Jaron.

"Say less," he replied.

Like a bat out of hell, Bilaal pulled up on his goons, ready to hold street court. Blyss had life and bullshit misconstrued if he thought shit was sweet. Watching Beautii find comfort in Blyss' arms made Bilaal feel as if his soul had just been ripped out of his chest. The savage in him wouldn't allow him to shed another tear, even though inside, he felt defeated. Instead, his sadness morphed into blind aggression and rage.

"What's good my nigga?" Leo greeted, as soon as Bilaal got out of his car.

"Ain't shit, my boy. Where everybody at?" Bilaal quizzed, after dapping his boy up.

"They in the house. Everything good?"

"Yeah, I need to holla at all y'all together," Bilaal said, jogging up the stairs with Leo.

Walking in the house, Moe was counting money, Keece was bagging up some dope, and Ray was bagging up a few guns and product for distribution.

"What up, B!" Keece, Moe, and Ray yelled out the minute they saw Bilaal.

"We got a problem," Bilaal cut straight to the chase.

"Aw shit! Who we gotta kill?" Keece asked. Everybody know his trigger finger stayed on go at all times.

"Oh I'ma be the one to do the killing this time, but I need y'all to help me figure out the smartest way to take this muthafucka down." Bilaal said.

"Who is it?" Moe questioned.

"Nigga named Blyss Valentino. He's a well known-"

"The best Lawyer in the whole state of California! Muthafucka is you crazy?" Ray cut Bilaal off and asked.

"Nah, but you gon' think you are after this ass whoppin' you gon' get, if you don't help me."

"The hell that man do to you?" Leo asked.

"He fuckin' my bitch." Bilaal huffed.

"Who? Willow?" Leo shot back, doing his best to hold back his laughter.

"Hell nah, Beautii." Bilaal answered.

"Damn man. How'd you find her?" Leo asked.

"It's a long ass story for another day. For now, I need all y'all to get your heads in the game. We can't afford to have no hiccups. We gotta execute this shit right, 'cause if we don't, we all going to prison for life.

"Mannn, you askin' a lot from a nigga for real. You know usually I'm down to ride, but this shit feel like a suicide mission. This man is a whole fuckin' attorney." Ray hesitantly reminded.

"Muthafucka, did I ask you al'lat?" Bilaal step in Rays face and based. "That nigga is a man just like me. He can be touched. He will be touched! I'on give a fuck what measures, or extremes I gotta go to." Bilaal announced to his soldiers.

"Aye' man, I'm just sayin'. Shit, all these women in the world, and you doin' all this over some pussy?" Ray looked Bilaal square in the eyes and asked.

"My pussy. My property. My possession!" Bilaal angrily spat.

Ray nodded his understanding. "A'ight, B, you got it."

"I know I got this shit. Now sit y'all asses down, and let's get a fuckin' plan together. Blyss Valentino gon' have to see me 'bout mine, real shit." Bilaal pulled out his cell phone and scrolled to Beautii's contact, then opened her message thread.

*Bilaal:*
*It'll be a cold day in hell before I give up on us. You're mine, and I'm steppin' ten toes down behind you.*
*Beautii:*
*You really need to let this go. If you love me, then let me be happy.*
*Let me go.*
*Bilaal:*
*You don't mean that shit. Don't say that shit no more. I love you.*

Bilaal backed out of the message thread, then refocused his attention towards his crew. He had a million and one thoughts and emotions shooting through his mind like lightning. He was so deep into the illusion he'd created in his head he couldn't rationalize or reason with anything contrary to what he envisioned. Confused was a major understatement. Delusional was putting it mildly. Demented was more like it. His thoughts, actions, feelings, and emotions had been so out of order for so long it became a part of his character.

    Bilaal was a man who thrived off of controlling people, places, and things. Beautii was a loose cannon that he couldn't control. Her mouth was reckless at times, she did her own thing, and didn't need him for shit. Bilaal had a love-hate relationship with Beautii's independence. His love for Beautii derived from an emotional co-dependency that was tapped into when Beautii accepted him for who he was. However, every woman should understand that a man who can't control his dick, can't control his energy; uncontrolled energy equals sporadic thoughts. If a man can't control his own reality, he's not fit to guide any woman through life when he can't see clearly.

## CHAPTER TEN

### BEAUTII HAMILTON

*A Few Weeks Later…*

Contemplative, pensive thoughts raced through Blyss' mind after a twelve hour work day. While he would have loved to end the day with Beautii, he understood time was of the essence. Despite the changes Blyss made in his life, that didn't negate his street sense. A few things were certain, nevertheless. Never leave loose ends, always take threats seriously, move in silence, and don't get caught slipping. Being proactive and keeping his word had always been strong suits for Blyss. He wasn't like a lot of people who give several opportunities for a muthafucka to play in his face. First impressions were the only impressions, and there were five things Blyss didn't play about. His freedom, his time, his energy, his money, or his woman. The slightest offset could cost a person their life.

Beautii had swept in Blyss' life, and became his Bonnie. They were connected on every level, and that was highly unlikely in 2023. Marriage and kids wasn't something Blyss looked forward to in the past; lately it'd become a constant consideration. This train of thought concluded Blyss' decision. The look in Bilaal's eyes was the only notification needed. Realizing that he was willing to go to this length for Beautii solidified how inclined his heart truly was. Anybody could get it.

Prior to getting off work, Blyss had sent a group text to his crew using their code word for emergencies. *Code Red/8:30 pm*. Everybody had responded and knew to be in place on time, no exceptions. Pulling over to stop at the gas station, Blyss exited the car to purchase a blueberry Red Bull and the blue pack of skittles for extra energy. It was one helluva combination to say the least, but it was like that sometimes. After purchasing, Blyss hopped back in the car, and shot Beautii a quick text.

*Blyss:*
*I'm thinkin' 'bout you, Beautiful.*
*Beautii:*
*Come see me?*
*Blyss:*
*After tonight, you ain't never gotta ask again. I got a late meeting.*
*Beautii:*
*Understood. Do what you gotta do, but when you finish… My door is open, come lay with me.*
*Blyss:*
*I got cha.*

Blyss hated that he had to tell Beautii a half truth, but Blyss saw things from a different perspective of clarity. When it came to reinforcing Beautii's security and the protection of her peace, everything he was doing was to reinforce it. Blyss was a lawyer, so he knew how to lie well for his clients, but he didn't allow that trait to flow into his personal life. Blyss understood the concept of not volunteering information that wasn't asked for the greater good. As he pulled out into traffic, he turned the volume up the second he heard the beat drop to *Sleazy Flow*.

It took Blyss about an hour to make it across town to Grind Park, a small suburban city they didn't go to unless it was truly necessary. Pulling up to the house, Blyss was glad everybody had made it on time, and before him. Wasting no time, he got out of the car, then secured the locks.

"What's good, fam?" Chief spoke to Blyss as soon as he made it through the front door.

"I can't call it, Chief. I 'preciate you comin' out on such short notice." Blyss returned, as Chief secured the door.

"What up, bro?!" Flex looked up from pouring everybody a double shot of cognac on the rocks.

"Man, it's been a long ass, eventful day." Blyss replied. "Where Screw at?"

"You already know a nigga ain't never to far away." Screw announced as he walked out of the bathroom, with his hand out."

"Nigga, did you wash yo hands?" Chief quizzed, and caused everybody to bust out laughing.

"Fuck you! Don't even try to play me like that." Screw defended himself.

"Y'all crazy as hell, man." Blyss stated, as he pulled out a chair and then sat at the head of the table. As he was the mastermind spearheading the operation. Since the first day he crossed paths with Bilaal, he'd hired a private investigator to bring him back every single thing he could possibly obtain on him. Blyss was aware of Bilaal watching, following, and researching him from day one. Timing was everything, and Bilaal wasn't worth risking all he'd worked so hard for. After gathering all the information necessary, the only thing that was unknown was how often Bilaal was watching him and Beautii. It didn't matter because today was the day it would all come to an end.

Blyss pulled out a white envelope that entailed a picture of Bilaal and his goons, their routine location, and three burner phones. Sliding them to the middle of the table, he informed his partners in crime. "I need y'all to ride to this address and bring this man to me alive." Blyss pulled the picture out of the envelope, then pointed at Bilaal. "I don't give a fuck who gets caught up in the cross fire. Do what you gotta do, and make it back as soon as possible." Blyss told his people. "This shit is personal, fam. Don't leave no witnesses, tie every loose end, and I'll be here when you get back." Blyss naturally gave direction and delegated responsibilities to his men. "Take Biggie and Quick with y'all to make sure it's a clean sweep, and no evidence is left behind when you leave." Blyss needed to ensure everyone's protection, and that this crime would become another unsolved mystery.

Without question, they all moved like soldiers due to the oath they'd taken years ago. They all knew if Blyss was asking them to do this, it had to be a reason. They trusted each other and were down to ride no matter the consequences.

*Three Hours Later...*

Creeping up the block, dressed in all black, hands covered in black gloves, and all faces were shielded by black masks; only revealing their eyes. Chief circled the block a few times to show everybody where the car would be parked at, and to let everybody out of the car at different angles of the house. The plan was to do a sneak attack, and catch them off guard. From the amount of evidence Blyss had produced on Bilaal and his goons, there was no doubt that they were indeed criminals, but they were moving sloppy as hell.

    Chief parked the car, killed the engine, then screwed the silencer on the end of his gun. Exiting the car, Chief swiftly disappeared in the darkness, and made his way to what appeared to be a trap house. After quietly meeting up with the crew, Screw kicked the back door down on the count of three, with their guns already drawn. Four naked women were in the kitchen cooking dope, while King Von's *All These Nigga's* pumped through the house speakers loudly.

*Pst. Pst. Pst. Pst…*

Shots were fired without a second thought. Zero fucks were given when it came to executing their mission. No witnesses could be left behind, and there was no telling how many people were downstairs that they would have to war with before getting to the one they were really there to get. Bilaal.

    "Yo! The fuck goin' on up here," Ray yelled as he reached the top of the stairs. *Pst…*

    Flex fired quickly, and knocked Ray back down the stairs. In less than a minute, every room was checked and cleared. Chief wasn't worried about anyone escaping because Biggie secured the back of the house, while Quick secured the front. Screw quickly peeked around the banister, and instantly noticed that no one noticed Ray laid on the ground, dead in a puddle of his own blood.

    Like an army, Chief, Screw, and Flex ran down the steps with their guns drawn. They'd studied the blueprint of the house during the ride, so they knew what door to go through to find Moe, Keece, and Bilaal.

Chief kicked down the door, with his gun drawn, as Chief and Screw followed closely behind him.

"What the hell is goin' on. Who the fuck sent y'all?" Bilaal quizzed, as his life flashed before his eyes. Throughout the years, he'd accumulated so many enemies, he had no clue who had the guts to try him. "Y'all bold enough to break into my shit, reveal yourself." Bilaal challenged, in utter disbelief.

*Pst. Pst.*

Flex and Chief executed a kill shot that brought Bilaal down to his knees. Crimson plasma splattered on the wall, and the pavement beneath them, as their souls instantly left their body.

"Ahhh! No, No, No, Noooo!" Bilaal broke down at the sight of his two best friends' lifeless bodies, and the realization that Ray was dead as well. There was no way that the masked intruders were able to get downstairs without bypassing Ray, who'd just went upstairs to see what had fallen on the floor. Little did they know, nothing had fallen; it was the door being kicked in.

"Get up slow, hoe ass nigga!" Chief demanded.

With his hands raised above his head, Bilaal raised from the ground. Repulsed by the ambush, and incapacitated mentally; his heart deflated as he stood to face his aggressors flat-footed in a huge oasis of his friends blood. Noxious were the intent of Bilaal's heart if he found his way through such a catastrophic situation. "Who the fuck sent you?" Bilaal hissed.

"Don't ask me shit nigga! Just walk ya happy ass around this table slowly, and keep yo fuckin' hands up!" Chief ordered, without a slither of remorse. He didn't have the capacity to commiserate.

Complying with what he was told, Bilaal rounded the table slowly, until he was standing face to face with Chief. With squinted eyes, Bilaal did his best to recognize Chief through his eyes; he drew a blank. Bilaal's reality had instantly dwindled into shit. He had nowhere to run, no one to call. If it were at all possible, he would have excavated a hole big enough to sink down into. "Just kill me," Bilaal spat, as he was completely over the suspense of the whole charade.

"Bitch, if your hoe ass was in control of some shit, you wouldn't be in this position would you?" Chief replied, with a hint of laughter in his tone.

Screw pulled a pair of handcuffs out of his back pocket, and squeezed them so tight around Bilaal's wrist, there was no doubt about his circulation being completely cut off.

"Ahhh!" Bilaal yelled. "Loosen these fuckin' cuffs. I know you ain't no fuckin' cop."

Flex stepped up, and patted Bilaal down. He removed three guns from his person, then confiscated his full clip of money; it appeared to be around ten bands.

"Yo' ass really about to rob this nigga at a time like this?" Chief shook his head, and Screw cracked up laughing.

Flex grabbed the duck tape from his other pocket, and sealed Bilaal's mouth shut so he couldn't make a scene once they got outside. "Let's go."

Once everyone made it to the hallway, Ray's soulless body was spiraled out on the floor. The weight of grief that rested on Bilaal's heart was nearly unbearable, heavy enough to knock his stance from solid to precarious. Bilaal managed to take weighted steps 'til he made it to the top of the stairs.

Looking around, everything seemed to still be in the same place as it had always been. When he reached the kitchen, Bilaal recognized Kisha, Trinity, and Taniah's naked bodies dead across the kitchen floor with bullet holes in the middle of their skulls. The dope they were cooking had burned on top of the stove, but apparently someone had turned it off before the smoke detector had a chance to go off.

"Take your shoes off," Chief ordered, noticing that Bilaal was tracking blood through the kitchen with his shoes. Taking the top off the *chloroform*, Chief made Bilaal inhale it; instantly knocking him out.

*Two Hours Later…*

Once Bilaal came back to himself after being sedated by *chloroform*, dismal energy, vile emotions, and incredulity hung over the Bilaal's head like a nimbus cloud. Bilaal's head spun like a tornado, and throbbed from a heinous headache. None of that stopped the odious plight that relentlessly formed in the pit of Bilaal's stomach the second he recognized Blyss' face.

"What up, gangsta?" Blyss jested purposely to piss Blyss off further. "You was walking pretty heavy the day you fraudulently walked into my place of business attempting to test me, and get at my woman. I hope you didn't think that shit was gon' fly."

Bilaal laughed. "Fuck you!"

"Nah," Blyss said calmly. "You wanted to fuck my woman again, but you couldn't even do that shit right. Tried to sneak back in her life, thinkin' she was the same woman she was when she walked away from yo' sorry ass. Tell me how it felt watchin' the woman you love, make love and give love to another nigga outside of you?"

"You're a dead man walkin', pussy." Bilaal gritted.

"I'm a dead man walkin', but you're sitting across from me bound by shackles, and at my mercy," Blyss viciously sneered. "Youz a bitch ass, counterfeit gangsta. You ain't 'bout shit, and you dumb as fuck my nigga. If you was half the nigga you pertray to be, there's no way I ever should have been able to get to you this easy. By the time yo' dumb ass attempted to look into who the fuck I was, I knew who yo' mama, granny, and great granny is, and their exact location in Virginia. I know where you rest your head at night, and where ya baby mother lives. How did your quest go with tryna find out where I lay my head at night tho?" Blyss chuckled. "The only man gon' die tonight is you." Blyss said, then grabbed a black sock full of rocks, and used it to knock Bilaal's front four teeth out of his mouth.

"Ahhh!" Bilaal exclaimed. "Just kill me!"

Preposterous was the thought of absolving anything with Bilaal when his understanding was so obtuse. Men like Bilaal didn't know what to do with second chances, they walked around with chips on their shoulders; as if they were owed something. They didn't realize that love and loss was a part of life. Their perceptions were so deplorable and distorted that therapy alone wasn't enough, only God could fully deliver them. Unfortunately, Blyss didn't have time to wait, and he acknowledged that the kill or be killed situation predicament presented required him to decide Bilaal's fate.

Blyss was a good man with a heart of gold, but Beautii; she was celestial in Blyss' eyes. There wasn't one thing Blyss wouldn't do to make her happy, and insure her safety at all cost. The responsibility Blyss accepted when he made Beautii his woman was paramount, and he took it to heart. Equivalent to a light switch, the look in Blyss' eyes instantly went from light to dark in mere seconds. Blyss resurrected his murderous nature that had been buried years ago, and grabbed the gun out of his holster on his side.

In his mind, Bilaal said his final prayer, as his whole life flashed before his eyes. A single tear fell from his right eye the moment he saw Beautii's smiling face in his mind.

*Pst. Pst...*

Blyss took two kill shots, one to the heart, and one in the center of his skull. Turning around, Blyss handed his gun to Chief, and nodded his head. They knew what needed to be done next.

"A'ight bruh. Holla at a nigga in the a.m." Chief told Blyss on his way out.

"I got cha." Blyss replied.

---

It was a quarter 'til three in the morning, and Blyss had just made it through Beautii's front door. To say the day had been eventful was a huge understatement. Blyss could have arrived about an hour earlier, but he needed to go home and take a shower first. Securing the door behind himself, Blyss slid his shoes off at the door. He sluggishly began his trail up the stairs, and down the hall that led to Beautii's room.

Tink's *Can I* streamed lowly from the small speakers in Beautii's room. She was sleeping like a baby when Blyss arrived. Inwardly, he swore up and down, she'd put a spell on him. There was no way she was this beautiful while she slept. Black bonnet on her head and all. Before climbing in the bed with Beautii, Blyss removed his gray sweats, briefs, and white t-shirt. The sweet notes of her perfume sent signals to Blyss like pheromones. Completely aroused, Blyss inched closer, gently pulling the covers back. Getting an eye full of Beautii's naked physique, Blyss was reminded of the fiend Beautii had turned him into.

"Hey babe," Beautii spoke softly, instantly opening her legs.

"Umm. What's good, bae," Blyss replied between the trail of kisses he made from her lips down to her middle. "Fuck, baby, this pussy is made of liquid crack," Blyss said, then licked her pussy like an ice cream cone. "Mmm," Blyss moaned, as shiverers raced up and down his spine. His tongue swiveled like a zigzag up and down Beautii's clit, instantly causing her stomach to tighten, and her body to jerk. Blyss made her pussy comply within seconds of the tongue lashing he was putting on her.

"Oooh, baby. Ssss. I'm cumming again." Beautii announced before exploding on Blyss' tongue.

Kissing his way up from Beautii's center, Blyss worked his way up to her stomach, all the while manipulating both Beautii's fudge areolas with his fingers. "You ready for me to work that lil' pretty pussy over, Beautii?"

"Yes. Please fuck me good, Blyss. Don't take it easy on me either. I want you to own this pussy tonight 'cause it belongs to you."

"Oh, I plan to do that and so much more," Blyss said, as he thrusted inside her, filling her up with one stroke.

"Ahh," Beautii moaned, until Blyss covered her mouth with his, and continued to go deeper and deeper.

*"Lord, You are an amazing God. I appreciate all the blessings and favor you've bestowed on my life. I'm grateful for how far you've allowed me to come, and the prosperity you've attached to everything I've set my mind to do. You've been faithful, and you've never let me down. I need You to remove anything from my life that's meant to drain me, weigh me down, or take me back to a place of stagnancy. Surround me with your grace, mercy, and real love. Amen.*

Beautii genuinely prayed as she stood in front of the window in her kitchen, gazing at the mesmerizing oasis, and drank a cup of hot tea. This was often the place she came to when she wanted to reminisce on where she came from, reflect on lessons learned, and renew her mind. It had been a long time since Beautii's mind drifted to thoughts of Bilaal. He was one man she wished she'd never got involved with, but she'd be lying if she said she didn't appreciate the things she learned about herself during their relationship. It didn't always feel good being with Bilaal, but Beautii learned how to honor herself. The truth was, no matter what place in life Beautii was in, she was worthy, and deserved love even at her lowest. There were several times Beautii wanted to give up, but she didn't.

 Beautii took responsibility and held herself accountable for the times she immobilized Bilaal and was the source of his emotional support. Now that she'd moved forward, Bilaal was still stuck. Not because he loved her, but because she'd filled such a prominent space in his heart and mind. So much to the point, it had become unhealthy, and felt like bondage to her. Beautii had to learn how to create peace with pieces, find joy in moments, meaning in the midst of silence, stillness in chaos, and perfection despite imperfections. There was a whole lot of life between heartbeats, and the resilient side of Beautii caused her to press beyond what seemed impossible. She fought to become the woman she had become, and nothing or no one was worth her losing herself again for.

"Lord, release me from this burden," Beautii whispered to God.

"Good morning, Babe. Did you rest well last night?" Blyss snuck up behind Beautii and asked, wrapping his arms around her waist from behind. "This view is magical, just like you."

"Hey you!" Beautii replied, as she nuzzled her head in the crook of Blyss' neck. His embrace was always so cozy, warm, and protective. "Thanks for coming to be with me, I tried hard to stay awake. I don't even remember when I fell asleep."

"It's cool. I knew how to wake you up," Blyss tittered, then kissed her neck. "Do you have plans for tonight?"

"No, not at all. What's going on?" Beautii turned to face him, instantly wrapping her arms around Blyss' neck, and pulling him closer.

"I wanna take you somewhere new tonight. You know, show you a different side of me." Blyss bore into her eyes and said.

"Count me in," Beautii pecked his lips, then stepped out of his embrace. "Before I do anything, I need to clean this house first. You wanna help?"

"Umm, you know I can call someone over here to clean for you," Blyss suggested. "Then we could go out for brunch."

Beautii laughed. "If my mother heard you say that, she'd

give you an ear full. I can hear her mouth fussing now from the first and last day my dad suggested the same thing you just did." Beautii smirked. "For now, you can go lay across my bed and wait for me. I still have a few things I wanna do to you before I get started."

"Oh yea?"

"Yea."

"Say less."

*Eight Hours Later…*

Blyss and Beautii walked into Erotic X-Stacy Dance Studio. Beautii wore a sexy red dress, gold accessories, paired with Black and gold stilettos. Blyss wore black Armani slacks with a black designer button down collar shirt and loafers. Beautii was astonished as she looked around, and observed the vibe of the club they'd entered. She never witnessed anything like it before. There were rooms where dance instructors were teaching people how to do several dances. The names of the classes were stationed on the outside of the doors, and open to anyone who wanted to join in. People from numerous nationalities were present with nothing but smiles on their faces. Some of the rooms had normal lights on and you could see everything going on from outside the door. However, what caught Beautii's attention was the room with the lights turned down low, that had the word *Kizomba* labeled beside the door.

"Let's see what's going on in here," Beautii pointed straight ahead to the *Kizomba* room.

"I knew I was drawn to you for a reason," Blyss said, as a smirk crept on his face.

Beautii giggled. "Why you say that?"

"This is the class I wanted to take you to," Blyss revealed.

"Not many people know about Kizomba, much less try to learn it because it's not easy to keep up."

"And you can keep up?" Beautii challenged.

"It's been said, if you can't fuck, you have no business even trying to do this dance. You guaranteed to fuck it up," Blyss explained. "Shit, you already know a nigga know how to fuck. You want another trial run before we go in?" Blyss manishly quizzed, silently daring Beautii.

"I'll take you up on that offer later. Right now, I wanna see what this dance is all about." Beautii winked her eye and said. Blyss opened the door, then smacked Beautii's ass as she walked through the door.

Dj Bleu was bumping *Keep It Right There* by Trey Songz, as a couple danced together front and center as everyone stood back and watched. Blyss watched Beautii, as she watched in awe of the movements. Jack and Jill were doing their thing, as they always did. They had perfected the art of the Kizomba dance, and now they specialized in putting an urban twist to it. The ultimate goal was to attract more melanin people, and the quickest way to do that is by playing music that catered to the melanin community.

Standing back a bit, Blyss watched as Beautii honed in, and began to mimic Jill's movements. He was impressed at how quickly she was catching on. The sexy movements of her waist, and the on time cross movements of her legs and feet moving in unison to the rhythm of the song. Once again, Blyss was mind blown at Beautii's ability to be diverse, and appreciate culture and art.

Deciding to try his hand, Blyss asked. "You wanna give it a shot? You think you can keep up?"

"I'm a good follower when I need to be," Beautii accepted his offer, and pulled Blyss a little closer before whispering into his ear. "And, I know how to fuck too." Beautii smiled seductively. "I'm ready whenever you are."

Blyss nodded and accepted the challenge. "We up next. I already reserved our time, and song. Beautii and Blyss continued to dance together as Beautii continued to watch Jill. She'd run across Kizomba a few times at home, so she wasn't a complete stranger to it. What they were about to do; however, would be the first time she'll be doing it in front of other people. She wasn't mad at it because if there was anyone in the world she'd want to dance with, it would be Blyss Valentino.

As soon as the song went off, the DJ called Blyss and Beautii to the dance floor. "Y'all make some noise for Blyss Valentino, and Beautii Hamilton!"

The crowd showed so much love as the duo made their way to the center of the floor. The beat dropped for Ashanti's *2:35 (I Want You)*, and sensually Blyss and Beautii came together. Automatically, their bodies rhythmically moved fluidly, as if they were teapots pouring into each other. Smooth, steady, sexy, and intentional movements is how they started off. While Kizomba is much like the tango, the subtle, yet intense way the hips fluctuate back and forth, and in circular motions sets this dance apart. Kizomba enables people to find their tempo within the song, and step with the off-beat of the song. The influence of Ashanti's voice allowed them to own the oasis of happiness they discovered in the warmth of each other's presence.

Everyone in the room stood back and marveled at the way Blyss and Beautii moved off pure energy and trust. After two years of building a solid work relationship, Beautii hadn't pegged Blyss as a man who could dance his ass off. Whoever said doing Kizomba was like having sex with your clothes on hadn't told one lie, and based on the small oasis Beautii made in her lace panties, as Blyss made her clit pulsate; made Beautii a believer.

As the song ended, Blyss pressed his lips against Beautii's with so much passion, he sent chills sprinting down her spine. Everyone stood around clapping and cheering. However, what Blyss didn't expect to see when he looked up, was Sedora standing off to the side on the verge of a breakdown. Somehow she manages to bat away the tears that threatened to fall from her eyes. Although she and Blyss had an agreement, the sight before her was both poignant and mesmerizing at the same time. This was the most inopportune time to run into Sedora, especially after the way things ended the last time Blyss had asked her to leave his office. It wasn't possible for him to duck the inevitable he saw coming from a mile away.

Sedora took a deep breath, then headed in Blyss and Beautii's direction. She repelled the sight of the duo she'd seen dance the night away, but she had to try her hand one more time before writing all the time she spent with Blyss throughout the years as a loss.

"Ehm," Sedora cleared her throat modestly, causing Beautii to turn around to face her. "Hi, I'm Sedora. An old friend of Blyss'." She introduced herself, and extended her hand. "Hey Blyss, can I speak to you for a minute?"

"Sedora, this is my woman, and business partner, Beautii Hamilton. Whatever it is that you need to say, you can speak freely in front of her." Blyss wasn't with the bullshit, and if Sedora thought she was about to expose anything, she had another thought coming.

"It's nice to meet you, Sedora. I love your shoes," Beautii complimented.

"Blyss, it'll be really quick, and I'd feel a little more comfortable speaking to you in private." Sedora pressed.

"Hey babe, I don't mind if you talk to her. She seems to have something really important to say." Beautii insisted.

"Hell nah, babe. Listen, I can't even call Sedora my ex because we never officially dated before. I've slept with her more times than I can count, but all those times were before you and I became official. We've had a contract in place for years now, but lately Sedora has been feeling like she can break it whenever she feels like it," Blyss revealed. "Now whatever you need to say, speak now or forever hold your peace."

"Oh, so this is where we are now, Blyss?" Sedora couldn't believe how Blyss had snatched the rug from underneath her.

"Look, I really wanna see you happy, but I just can't be the one to do it. I feel it's best for you to walk away, because I'm all in with my lady. I honestly don't have it in me to lie, or lead either of you on. Beautii is my choice, Sedora, and I apologize if it hurts you to hear my truth," Blyss empathized. "There's someone out there who deserves you, and who'd appreciate all that you bring to the table. You're a phenomenal woman… be that for the right man."

Sedora quickly wiped the tears that escaped her eyes, then nodded her understanding as she walked away.

"Beautii I apolog-"

"Shhh." Beautii pressed her finger against Blyss' lips, then wrapped her arms around his neck. "I've always respected the man you are, but after that, my respect level just soared through the roof. Come make love to me again on this dance floor."

"Alright, you keep on and I'ma have yo' ass bent over upstairs in a private room."

# CHAPTER ELEVEN

## BLYSS VALENTINO

*B*eautii was delighted to finally see where "Thee Blyss Valentino" rested his head at night. Never in her life had she ever stepped inside of a home as immaculate as his. The outside alone was fit to be on the cover of somebody's luxury homes magazine. Stepping over the threshold, everything was top tier from the marble floors, expensive chandeliers, and fancy staircase; to the high-end luxury furniture. Beautii loved the warm vanilla and soft brown color scheme throughout the home. All-consuming were the feelings of solace and security. Much like Blyss' personality, his home felt down to earth, yet rich at the same time. The atmosphere gave a relaxed vibe that instantly made Beautii feel at home.

Sitting in Blyss' jacuzzi looking up at the high ceiling, Beautii was at complete peace. The scent from the Vanille candle by Diptyque traveled and filled the space around them tastefully, as Blyss sat across from her gently massaging her feet, and wrapping his tongue around her toes.

"Umm, yes Blyss. That feels so good," Beautii moaned, enjoying every second of being loved down by her man.

"All that dancing you did tonight, I figured your feet needed some attention." Blyss replied.

"You're so sweet. So good to me."

"I'm just gettin' started."

"So, what about tonight made you feel it was the right opportunity to bring me to your home for the first time?"

"I've been contemplating the decision for a while, but I needed to be sure."

"Hmm. So, what was the deciding factor?"

Blyss released Beautii's foot back in the water before responding. "To be real with you, it was when I made love to you for the first time without a contract in place, and with no protection. A nigga like me don't trust easily when it comes to my livelihood, my image, and most importantly my heart. With you, everything is just different. It feels authentic and new." Blyss explained. "When I realized there was no length I wouldn't go to, in order to ensure your safety; I knew we were soulmates. Seeing you happy, evolving, thriving, and becoming all you were created to be, makes me happy." Blyss told her truthfully.

*God, what did I do to deserve this man?* Beautii questioned God in her mind. "You always seem to know what I need to hear. How is that?" Beautii quizzed with a raised brow.

Blyss snickered. "It definitely ain't rehearsed. That's all I do is speak from the heart. My mom told me a long time ago that, when I found the one, there would be no denying it."

"So, you feel like I'm the one? Please elaborate."

"She said I wouldn't be able to deny it, and when I opened my mouth, my heart would speak its truth, without my mind's permission. And, she ain't neva lied. Not one time have I questioned my feelings, emotions, actions, or words when it comes to you. It all aligns. I don't give everybody that kind of access to me. As a matter of fact, no one has the access you have to me; except God and my mama."

Beautii sat there for a few seconds, speechless. She didn't know what to say after Blyss' admittance. The truth was despite the love she received from both her parents, in the past she consistently attracted the wrong type of men. Blyss was a real man, and his timing couldn't have come at a better time. *This is my reward.* She was ready to receive him. Beautii had prayed, prepared, and positioned herself, and Blyss poured into her just as much as she poured into him. She couldn't ask for a better man to spend time and share space with. "Thank you for choosing me."

Standing up, and stepping out of the jacuzzi, Blyss wrapped a towel around himself. "Come show me how thankful you are." Blyss suggested.

Without another word, Beautti gladly stepped out behind Blyss, dried off, then met him in his bedroom. Once she stepped back inside Blyss' room, he had several gift bags sitting on top of the bed waiting for Beautii. "Oh my God, Blyss! What is all of this?"

"Just a few things I picked up for you. Come look inside the bags," Blyss insisted.

Hurriedly, Beautii made her way across the room, and sat on the bed, so she could see what was inside the bags. She started with the *Icebox* bag. "This is beautiful, Blyss. I love it." Beautii gushed, as she admired the jewelry set he'd gotten her. Reaching for the bag that said, Oasis Press, Beautii pulled out a maroon colored box, and quickly removed the lid. Beautii's eyes landed on a custom made book with a picture she took with Blyss, two years ago when they first started working together.

## Infinite, Timeless, Love... Beautii & Blyss 🖤

Beautii's eyes glazed over, tears at the brim of her eyes; she was in utter disbelief with his ability to be so creative. No one outside of her parents and fayth had ever taken the time to do anything to this magnitude for her. Beautii beamed as she flipped through the pages. There was no way she could possibly hide her satisfaction with such a small, but significant gift. Beautii was blown away when she made it to the back of the book, and realized there were pictures included from the day Blyss had dinner catered to her on the rooftop.

Beautii gasped. "How... Who took these?" Beautii inquired.

"Can't tell you all my secrets. Just know I'm all about capturing every moment possible when I'm with you." Blyss replied, genuinely. "But, that picture right there," Blyss pointed to the picture on the page, before Beautii flipped it. "That's one of my favorites in this whole book." Blyss said with a smile on his face. Blyss had a handful of Beautii's ass in one hand, gripping her waist with the other one, and his tongue swirling around Beautii's nipple. Beautii, on the other hand, had her eyes closed, back mildly arched backwards, as her left hand gripped the back of Blyss' neck, while her right hand rested on top of Blyss' heart.

Picking up the other small box that was right beside the custom book, Beautii opened it, and instantly shed the tears that had been begging to be released. There were seven hundred and thirty sticky notes filled with the sentiments of Blyss' heart written on paper. "How did you know?" Beautii asked.

"It's my job to know your love language. It's my endeavor

to know everything about you, Beautii." Blyss replied, then kissed her forehead.

Beautii loved spending time with Blyss, appreciated every touch she received from him, even anticipated his gifts because it's simply who he was; a giver. Words. Not just any words, but words that held depth, had meaning behind them, and heartfelt. Words of affirmation was Beautii's top love language, and the fact that Blyss knew, and understood this about her was worth more than riches and fine gold. Removing the gift tissues from the *Valentino* bags, Beautii loved the two designer dresses Blyss had purchased her with black *Valentino* stilettos to match.

Beautii bore deep into Blyss' soul, and dropped down to her knees. The way Blyss loved her down tore straight through her exterior walls, and exposed her vulnerability. Love was so powerful, so evident, and transparent between them; mere words would have diluted its potency.

Looking up from the ground, Beautii pulled at the towel that was wrapped around Blyss' waist. It tumbled down to the ground, along with her resolve. Reaching forward, Beautii took the tip of Blyss' dick and licked it like a watermelon flavored lollipop.

"Shit," Blyss surrendered to the passionate hypnosis Beautii had welcomed him into. Boring into his eye as she took him in deeper, drove Blyss wild. Instinctively, he grabbed the back of Beautii's head, and journeyed deeper down her throat.

Beautii relaxed her throat and gladly welcomed him in. Fluidly. Beautii fluently spoke Blyss language in return. Physical touch. It was apparent to her since the first time she'd done it. Beautii paid attention to everything about Blyss, his body language, responses to her during intimate moments, and his eyes. His eyes were always dead giveaways because they were gateways to Blyss' soul. His inner man was so beautiful, she looked forward to his raw exposure when she catered to him.

After a few minutes of watching Beautii's lips slide up and down his pole, he suddenly needed to bury his dick deep inside her oasis. Blyss gently tapped Beautii's shoulder, bit down on his bottom lip, then motioned with the chuck of his head for her to get up. She obliged, then naturally wrapped her arms around his neck once she stood. "What you tryna do to me?" Blyss quizzed.

"Be all you need and more, forever and always," Beautii answered.

"You already are," Blyss told her honestly. "I got one more thing for you."

"Are you serious? You've already given me so much, Blyss."

Stepping out of Beautii's embrace, Blyss walked over to his nightstand, and grabbed a normal sized white envelope. "I'ma spoil you with the finest things in life every chance I get for two simple reasons. You deserve it, and 'cause I want you to have it all."

Naturally, Beautii was a nurturer. She wasn't materialistic, but she loved surprises, and appreciated everything Blyss blessed her with. "That's why every time I'm with you, I give you my all. I don't ever wanna be without you, Blyss Valentino."

"The way a nigga been overdosing on you," Blyss pulled her back into his space. "I ain't never letting you go. Now, see what's in the envelope."

Beautii's eyes widened the size of two saucers when they landed on two tickets to Oasis Island. It was an island set apart, but not far from St. Croix. "Blyss, this fight leaves at two o'clock in the morning."

"It does."

"Well, how am I supposed to do-"

"Calm down. I've already taken care of everything," Blyss spoke softly, and calmed her nerves. "I've cleared our schedules for the rest of this week and next. Jillian has already called out clients, and rescheduled with the courts for our appearances. I just wanna be with you, Beautii. There's no use of making all this money, and having access to all these things; if I never make time to enjoy myself and those I care about."

Beautii pondered on Blyss' words, and agreed. "You're right. Now I have to go home and pack a bag, then come back."

"Your bags have already been packed," Blyss informed, then pointed to the designer bags sitting by the couch.

"You're too good to be true." Beautii said, wondering how she'd overlooked those bags that were clearly not luggage fit for a man.

"I'm as real as it get's. Now come bend that ass over."

"Gladly."

---

After hours of traveling, Beautii and Blyss finally made it to Oasis Island. Nothing but white sand, pretty blue water, and the most entrancing sunset she'd ever witnessed in her life. Beautii stood, cocooned in Blyss' strong arms, and drank fruit juice out of a small melon. Whitney Houston's *You Give Good Love* streamed from Beautii's Oasis playlist on her phone, as they appreciated the small break of silence between them. They were surrounded by good vibes, the atmosphere had been set. While Blyss had proven to be an alpha and a protector, Beautii was a natural nurturer. Since the moment their plane landed and the boat sailed into the island's shore, Beautii had been uncovering the layers of Blyss' heart. She wanted to embody his purpose, so she could push him to greater exploits. Beautii made it her mission to explore the deepest parts of his mind, because knowing him through and through was non-negotiable.

A safe haven. Beautii became just that for Blyss, and she would spend a lifetime loving him infinitely. Finally, Beautii was equally yoked with a man who matched her drive, and shared her heart. Blyss was the type of man all women held space for. He had all the right characteristics, respectable morals, and wanted to be all about his woman. Blyss was the type of man a good woman would be a fool to mishandle. There was no part of him that needed to be fixed, nothing to judge, and no inadequacies whatsoever. Blyss was deserving of unconditional love and support Beautii had to give. In her eyes, even his imperfections were perfect.

"Babe, you wanna play a game?" Beautii interrupted the brief silence and asked.

"A game? What kind of game?" Blyss replied, then took a sip of his cognac infused drink.

"Would you rather," Beautii turned to face Blyss and asked. "It's really simple and fun." Beautii excitedly stated with a smile.

"A'ight, you go first though," Blyss agreed.

Taking a few moments to think, Beautii asked. "Would you rather be a billionaire, but never find love, and have no respect. Or, would you rather live in the projects, with a million dollar idea, and find the love of your life?"

"Yo' lil' ass crazy," Blyss laughed, and thought about it for a minute. "I'ma go wit' option two because it's the one I relate to most," Blyss told Beautii honestly. "I got it out the mud,

Beautii. Wasn't shit handed to me. Everything I have, came with hard work, dedication, and discipline. I earned my respect in the streets, and in my profession. To be honest, I never opened myself up to love until I met you."

Beautii took in every word Blyss spoke like a sponge, and reserved it in her long-term memory. She didn't take it for granted when anyone revealed their heart to her, especially not Blyss. "I can definitely respect that. It's your turn now."

"Would you rather live on a secluded Island with sight, and no memories, and live a mediocre life. Or, have memories and no future sight or vision moving forward, but you're rich?" Blyss asked with a smirk on his face.

"What?! That's crazy. How I'm posed to choose from those pissy options?"

Blyss shrugged. "You the one wanted to play this crazy ass game." Blyss reminded then cracked up laughing.

Suddenly, Beautii felt nauseous and her stomach felt like it was in knots. With one hand covering her mouth, Beautii quickly sat her drink down and ran to the bathroom. It was a good thing that her hair was already pinned up, as she ejected everything she'd eaten for the last two days into the toilet bowl. She had no clue what hit her all of a sudden, but she felt like shit. Her head spun out of control, and everytime she thought she was finished throwing up, more came up until she dry heaved. Blyss stood by the door for a few minutes, and studied Beautii thoroughly before making a move. They hadn't been together long enough for him to know her menses cycle, but deep down in the core of his gut he knew.

Blyss proceeded forward into the bathroom, grabbed a face towel, and ran warm water on it. After ringing the towel out, he walked over to the toilet, where Beautti was down bad. "Come here, babe. Let me help you out."

"I... I don't-"

"Shhh, I got you. Let me get you cleaned up," Blyss insisted, refusing to allow Beautii to lift a finger as he catered to her. He washed her face, brushed her teeth, removed all her clothes, then got inside the shower and cleansed her body from head to toe. He even unpinned and washed Beautii's hair, then massaged her scalp with conditioner. Once again, Beautii hated to compare; but Bilaal could never compete. Blyss was on his grown man shit, and had raised the bar so high; it surpassed the sky.

*Three Hours Later...*

Beautii had fallen asleep, but was awakened to the smooth sound of K Camp's *Blessing* spilling from the surround speakers that was connected to the TV. Seconds later, Blyss walked through the door holding a tray of chicken and vegetable soup, with fresh juice, hot tea, water, and ginger ale. Blyss wasn't sure what Beautii felt up to drinking, but he wanted to give her options.

"I made you something to eat while you were resting," Blyss told Beautii as she sat up with her back against the headboard.

"How long was I sleep?" Beautii asked, and then yawned in her hand.

"Not long," Blyss replied, then set her tray up in front of her.

"Thank you for taking care of me. I don't know why I feel sick all of a sudden. I'll make a doctor's appointment once we get back to Groove City if this doesn't pass." Beautii still felt light headed, and nauseous.

"You'll be fine," Blyss winked, then sat on the side of the bed, and fed Beautii the soup he'd just made for her.

What Beautii and Blyss were experiencing together was truly an oasis of love. Love, like our Creator can't be housed in a box. It can't be restricted, limited, or controlled. True love often starts small, then blossoms overtime. One thing about an oasis, once it's witnessed, its presence can never be denied. Especially, when you've been through a drought. Life has a way of showing us when it's time for an oasis, Beautii and Blyss were just glad they were at the right place in time to receive what had already been written since the beginning of time.

# CHAPTER TWELVE

## BEAUTII HAMILTON

**Two Months Later**

"Blyss, you tryna be nasty. Your parents are coming over today, and I gotta make sure this food is right." Beautii playfully fussed. Beautii's parents loved Blyss, and she hoped to match the same amazing impression on Blyss' parents.

"I'on know why you trippin'. My parents gon' love you cause I do. Shit, their opinion really don't matter anyway. We already locked," Blyss hugged Beautii from behind, attempting to undo the drawstring tie in the front of her Nike sweats.

"Yea, that's easy for you to say." Beautii replied, as she pulled out some fresh greens from her refrigerator.

"Turn around and look at me," Blyss said seriously.

She obliged, quickly. "Blyss you are slowing down my process."

"I said I love you, Beautii." Blyss repeated.

Beautii had been moving so fast, she didn't hear Blyss the

first time he confessed his love for her. She never rushed him to say the four letter word, she figured he'd say it when he was ready. Without a second thought, Beautii replied. "I love you too, Blyss."

"Do you really?"

"Yes I do. I wouldn't say it if it wasn't true."

"I'm sayin' tho. If what we have is true, then things like trust, loyalty, and understanding comes with it too, right?"

"Of course, Blyss. Have I done anything to make you think otherwise?"

"No. I just want you to be yourself when my parents get here. You don't have to please them. I'm yo' man, and I'm pleased already. If anyone, parents included, have a problem accepting who I love, then they'll be cut off. Simple."

"What?" Beautii nervously laughed, although nothing was funny. "You'd really do that?"

"In a New York minute. You're my world, baby. I'ma fall out with anybody who even think they gon' come between us."

"I'd never make you choose."

"You'll never have to, my choice gon' always be you."

Beautii wrapped her arms around Blyss, and kissed him sweetly. "You're so good to me. God sprinkled something extra in the dust when he created you for me."

"Mhm, now can I get a lil bit?"

Beautii laughed. "As tempting as it sounds, the answer is no. I gotta get these pots jumping. You know you gon' wanna eat later on."

"Mannnn, a'ight. I'ma go ahead and get my clothes out and hop in the shower." Blyss said, then kissed Beautii's forehead.

Beautii changed her mind at the last minute and decided against making steak, and decided to make stuffed chicken breast, wild rice, and broccoli for the main course. Banana pudding would be the desert. Beautii wanted everything to be perfect because this would be the time for she and Blyss to announce their big news to his parents. They'd already told her parents the week prior. Grabbing her phone, she pressed play on her favorite playlist and got to work, because she knew how fast time would go by; she still needed to get dressed too. Blyss thought it'd be a good idea to have dinner at Beautti's house because he wanted his parents to see and feel what he did when he was in her comfort zone.

*Ding… Ding… Ding…*

Beautii sat two family packs of chicken breast down on the counter, then went to the door. *Who could this possibly be? I'm not expecting any company today. Lord, please don't don't let this be Mr. and Mrs. Valentino. I'm nowhere near ready.*

"Just a second. I'm coming," Beautii announced before opening the door. "Willow?" Beautii was beyond surprised. "What are you doing here?"

"A better question is, where the hell is Bilaal?" Willow sassed.

"Umm… I haven't seen Bilaal since the last time he showed up to my job begging me to be with him."

"Look, I don't have time for the bullshit. Y'all can live in a fantasy world all y'all want, but I got real life problems. Like who the fuck gon' help me take care of these gotdamn kids!"

Beautii was flabbergasted to say the least. So many questions raced through her mind, but she didn't have time to rationalize any of her thoughts. "Look, just hold on a second." Beautii closed her door, and ran back to the kitchen to get some cash out of her purse. She used her card for just about everything, but she made it her business to at least keep two hundred dollars on her at all times. Once she located it, she rushed back to the door.

"Here," Beautii handed Willow the two hundred dollars. " I don't know what kind of games are being played, but Bilaal isn't here. We are not in a relationship at all. I don't know what he told you, or how you know where I live." Beautii shook her head. "Now isn't a good time."

Here's my number, you need to call me as soon as you can," Willow said, then turned around and left.

*To be continued...*

# AFTERWORD

You made it to the end of the first installment of *Oasis*. I truly hope you enjoyed the love spilled on these pages, because Oasis Two is going to be nothing less than another strategic, love filled journey. Initially, I thought this book was going to be a quick novella for Valentine's Day. That is, until my characters notified me otherwise. They have a lot more to unpack apparently. Stay tuned- Oasis 2 is coming soon.

ABOUT AUTHOR AJA CORNISH:

*Aja Cornish was born October 6 in Chicago, Illinois, and is currently a native of Charlotte, North Carolina. She has obtained her Bachelor's degree in Psychology, and is currently in the process of receiving her Master's degree. She notes that her passion for writing started the day she was able to grip a pencil, however; her love for reading didn't bud until her eighth-grade year of middle school. Aja is extremely intentional about carving out her own lane,*

## ABOUT AUTHOR AJA CORNISH:

*mastering her craft, and leaving her imprint on the hearts of all who read and enjoy her art. Her debut novel "Restored Treasure" was published December 2020. She has eleven titles under her belt to date, and shows no signs of slowing down.*

*Aja says she was twenty-eight years old working as a correctional officer when she picked up her first urban fiction book by Wahida Clark. From there she delved deeper by reading other authors such as Ashley & JaQuavis, Keisha Ervin, Love Belvin, Nicole Jackson, Takerra Allen, BriAnn Denae, Charae Lewis and many more. Aja found pleasure and contentment in the escapes she received through the stories of all the characters she read about. She became an avid reader during a very hard time in her life, and the escapes she received kept her mind from being idle. Now that Aja has gained the courage to write her own books, it's her endeavor to create these same escapes for those who read and fall in love with her characters one word at a time.*

*Aja writes stories with depth. She gives her readers something they can feel, and think about long after her characters stop speaking. The gems dropped in her stories have the capacity to stand throughout time. For more information about Aja, she can be found at:*

## SOCIAL MEDIA LINKS:

*https://www.thefinestgems.co*
**_Facebook: The Finest Gems Reading Club_**
**_Facebook Author Like Page_**
Instagram: Author Aja Cornish
Twitter: @ajacornish

## ALSO BY AJA CORNISH

- *Restored Treasure*
- *The Days When Love Was Enough*
- *The Day Love Stopped Being Enough Pt.2*
- *Certainty*
- *Circumstances*
- *Enigma*
- *Things Change… But, Can The Marriage Handle it?*
- *When It Hurts The Most*
- *When It Hurts The Most Pt.2*
- *Disruption*
- *All I Want Is You: A Thanksgiving Short*
- *Give Me You: A Christmas Short Story*
- *Undone: A New Year's Short*
- *Galentine Gang*
- *Imprint On My Soul*
- *Now I See*
- *Irrevocably In Love: A Thanksgiving Short Story*
- *The Purest Love: A Christmas Short*
- Galentine Gang 2
- Forever I'm Yours